May's Moon:
Fortis Mission

May's Moon:
Fortis Mission

S. Y. Palmer

OUR STREET
BOOKS

Winchester, UK
Washington, USA

JOHN HUNT PUBLISHING

First published by Our Street Books, 2019
Our Street Books is an imprint of John Hunt Publishing Ltd., Laurel House, Station Approach,
Alresford, Hants, SO24 9JH, UK
office@jhpbooks.com
www.johnhuntpublishing.com
www.ourstreet-books.com

For distributor details and how to order please visit the 'Ordering' section on our website.

ISBN: 978 1 78904 091 3
978 1 78904 092 0 (ebook)
Library of Congress Control Number: 2018941702

A CIP catalogue record for this book is available from the British Library.

Design: Stuart Davies

UK: Printed and bound by CPI Group (UK) Ltd, Croydon, CR0 4YY
US: Printed and bound by Thomson-Shore, 7300 West Joy Road, Dexter, MI 48130

We operate a distinctive and ethical publishing philosophy in
all areas of our business, from our global network of authors to
production and worldwide distribution.

Dedication
To my family:
Thanks for the memories of yesterday, the fun of today
and our hopes for tomorrow.

Acknowledgement

To those who knew the second book would be difficult – thank you for saying nothing.

To those who had no idea – thanks for constantly asking, 'Have you finished yet?'

Chapter One

Click. The red arrow on the hatch door handle turned one hundred and eighty degrees to the word *Locked*. Michael May had imagined this moment for over half his life. In just minutes the launch sequence would commence and the fuel-packed rocket would thrust him into space. He looked down at his orange flight suit: an American emblem on one arm, a European badge on the other and a round *Fortis* mission patch on his chest. No more simulations. This time he was doing it for real.

The golden ball of Florida sun acted as a perfect spotlight, illuminating the historical event below. Banks of TV cameras trained their lenses on the spacecraft, crowds of excitable fans cheered and gangs of journalists interviewed nervous relatives. Only once had Michael glanced at his family. He couldn't bear to see the enormity of what he was about to do reflected in their faces. Whoops and shouts rang out as the 'five-minute countdown' announcement boomed over loudspeakers and a sea of photographers shouted for one last front page-worthy image.

Crammed into their crew capsule and wedged in their bucket seats, the six astronauts carried out their final suit checks and fastened their harnesses. Michael was less than four minutes away from being fired into the sky in a spacecraft that had never carried a crew before and five months earlier than scheduled. If anything went wrong, this thing contained enough fuel to give Florida the best firework display ever.

Michael scrunched up his clammy, gloved-hands, tried to ignore the thread of sweat zigzagging down his back and flicked up one of the tabbed switches at arm's length. 'Er...this is Michael May confirming my communication link.'

'Check,' said a voice to his left.

It was the pilot, Steve Winters. ' How are you doing, Michael?'

'Er...I'm OK thanks, Steve. I suppose I can't actually believe we're going. I mean...I've been thinking about this for years and now I'm suddenly sitting here.'

Steve smiled. 'It's a bit surreal, isn't it? I'm the same, even though it's my third mission. You've just got to repeat what we did in training and enjoy the ride. Just think about the best rollercoasters you've been on. You're excited and nervous before it starts. Then you scream and shout; but as soon as it's over, you want to do it all again.'

Michael nodded. His stomach was already flipping and plunging like a rollercoaster and they hadn't even left the ground.

Suddenly the spacecraft shuddered as if it was waking up for action, and then again more violently.

'Systems startup,' announced mission commander, Ralph Grant.

Michael closed his gloves around the edge of his seat as the booster rockets fired up. They were being shaken like a bone in a super-sized dog's mouth.

'*Inceptor 1*, this is John Dell at Mission Control. Do you copy?' said a voice in Michael's headset.

'Copy, John. This is Ralph Grant welcoming you to *Inceptor 1* on this glorious Florida morning. Awaiting further instructions and thirty-second countdown. We're good to go and excited to be taking *Inceptor 1* up to the International Space Station (ISS). Over.'

A second bang told Michael that the main engines were igniting. The fierce vibrations transformed the instrument panel in front of him into a blur of indistinct shapes.

'Thirty seconds to lift off,' announced Steve. 'All systems

checked and nominal.'

'Roger that,' said Ralph. 'Crew are harnessed and good to go. Mission Control, we are awaiting your countdown. Over.'

'*Inceptor 1*, this is John Dell at Mission Control. We are going into ten seconds countdown. Good luck, guys. We're all thinking of you and the world is watching.'

Michael's mum, dad and sister, Millie, flashed into his thoughts. They'd be outside in the sunshine with Granny May, who'd flown in from England just for the launch. He pictured his mum, hands over her mouth, Millie taking pictures to show her friends, Granny May covering her eyes, saying she couldn't watch and his dad grinning. Just for a split second, he wished he was down there with them, where everything was certain.

'Ten...nine...eight...seven...six...five...four...'

Michael breathed in slowly through his nose and then out through his mouth for as long as he could.

'Three...two...one...'

A metallic clang echoed in the capsule, followed by a neck-jarring shudder. The four robot-like arms, that held the spacecraft to the launch tower like a protective mother, released their grip and the fireball beneath propelled him upwards.

As the g-force kicked in, it was like the whole of his football team had suddenly jumped on top of him.

Bang! At two minutes, the solid booster rockets fell away. Michael tensed his abdomen as the pressure continued but he still had six more minutes to endure. He studied the readouts on the instrument panel and tried to lift his manual to check them, but it was as if his arm had been glued to his lap.

'Ninety seconds until shield jettison,' announced Ralph.

From his strained voice, Michael could tell that *Inceptor*

1's commander was feeling the overbearing pressure of the g-force too.

Bang! Another shudder rocked the capsule as light suddenly flooded in and the protective shields were jettisoned. *Inceptor 1*'s second stage engines burst into life just before the first stage tanks burned out and fell away.

But as quickly as the light arrived, it was smothered by darkness. The pressure on Michael's chest magically lifted and the roar quietened to a gentle hum. Now his body felt like a single piece of iron filing, being pulled upwards by a powerful magnet.

'Mission Control, this is *Inceptor 1*. Do you copy?' said Ralph.

There was a pathetic crackle over the communication link, but no voice.

'Mission Control, this is *Inceptor 1*. Do you copy?' he repeated.

Michael flicked a look at Steve. Was something wrong? A few more crackles like an asthmatic wheeze came across the link before he could make out faint voices.

'*Inceptor 1*, this is John Dell at Mission Control. Sorry, we lost our link for a few seconds. Glad to have you back and we can confirm successful first stage separation and perfect pitch manoeuvre. Congratulations, guys. You're the first crew to take *Inceptor 1* into orbit.'

Michael's arms prickled at these words. He was actually in space. Michael May, the boy they used to nickname 'Micky Moon' at home because of his obsession, had made it into orbit. He lifted his hands to his face like they were made of clouds. It was so easy.

'OK, guys. Well, I hope that was the ride of your lives,' said Ralph, smiling. 'Systems and pressure are nominal. Leak checks are complete and normal. Solar arrays are deployed. We're on for a short trajectory today but you've

got a little while before we start our approach, so take off
your gloves and helmets and enjoy.'

Michael looked at the rest of the crew. There was Sarah
Hutchins, who was the NASA mission specialist in charge
of scientific experiments. This was her third visit to the ISS.
Marat Orlov was an experienced Russian cosmonaut who
was the flight engineer and lunar module pilot. He didn't
say much but Michael respected his no-nonsense approach.
Ralph Grant was the mission commander from NASA and
was Michael's idea of the perfect astronaut. Patriotic, fit,
confident and not afraid to take control of a situation, he'd
been a military pilot for nearly twenty years. Steve Winters,
the only other British crew member, was *Inceptor 1*'s pilot.
He was also going to be part of the lunar crew with Marat
and Ralph. Finally, there was Sarah's assistant, the mission
specialist support. This was someone Michael knew better
than anyone else – someone who'd seen him through the
best and worst of times in training. His own age and with
a wicked sense of humour, it was Buddy Russell.

'Hey, Mike. How weird does this feel?' came Buddy's
voice from behind.

Michael nodded as he lifted his arm out in front of
him. It stayed there just like the rest of his body would
the second he released his harness. Slowly, a smile slid
from one side of his mouth to the other. After removing
his gloves and helmet, he pressed the triple harness lock
on his bucket seat, grabbed a rail on the ceiling and pulled
himself upwards. He moved clear of his seat and hovered
there. This was what most people called weightlessness
and something only real astronauts could do.

'Hey, Mike. Reckon my mom would love this, don't
you?' said Buddy, using the back of one of the seats to
spin himself around. With nothing to stop him, he kept
spinning, like he was on a fairground ride. 'No backache

when you're weightless, hey.'

'Yeah, she would,' replied Michael, lifting his knees up to his chest and pulling himself along the roof...or was it the floor now?

One by one the six astronauts rose out of their seats like cloth bubbles and into whatever position they wanted. Steve adopted a superman-type pose, whilst Ralph attempted a mid-air headstand and soon the capsule looked like a mass of clumsy octopus tentacles.

'Hey, let's get a picture for the guys back home,' said Ralph, taking a group photo.

'Nice hair, Sarah,' said Steve, pointing to her long, blond, wispy stalagmite strands.

'OK, guys,' said Ralph, interrupting the laughter. 'Enjoy this moment. Let's get a few more photos to send back home, complete our checks and then we need to get on. We've a space station to find and a mission to start.'

Michael stared out of his round window. Somewhere in all that darkness was a space station travelling at 17,500 miles an hour that was to be his home for the next two months. Could he do this? Could he live up here, so far away from everything and everyone he knew?

His circular view was an exact mirror of all the images he'd ever seen – a tiny, colourful sphere hovering in dense, impenetrable black. And somewhere on this artist's palette of brown, green, blue and white, were his family, friends and home.

Having made it into low orbit, the next challenge was to connect two spacecraft that were travelling at more than five miles a second in different directions.

'Imagine the earth is an orange,' Bob Sturton had explained in training. 'Then imagine two objects going around the orange in perfect circles, but around different parts of the orange. The biggest circle is around the middle of the orange; the other circles must be smaller. So two spacecraft travelling at the same speed will complete a circle of the orange at different rates depending on which part of the orange they are travelling around. That is the challenge of orbital mechanics.'

'Crew, prepare to begin our burns,' said Marat in his staccato voice. 'Return to your seats and re-harness.' Marat would decide how much they needed to move up or down to find the ISS and use short burns of *Inceptor 1*'s engine to alter their position.

With each successive burn, Michael strained for his first sight of the ISS. The house-sized, geometrical space construction that had cost a billion dollars to build and taken hundreds of space flights to construct had to be just behind him.

'Minor adjustments until docking,' said Marat. 'Approximately twenty-four minutes.'

Michael searched for a mass of spheres, canisters, beams and triangles. With solar panels of four thousand square feet on each side of the ISS, it looked like a mammoth, junk metal bird to him; not at all what he would have designed as a pioneering research centre and first proper home for astronauts.

Just then Michael saw a super bright dot, like a star. As he watched, the dot gradually grew to an uneven mass of lights. A few minutes more and the lights began to resemble a body with spider-like legs until finally, Michael recognised one of the legs as a solar array panel. Large enough to power ten homes, the panel tilted to absorb the sun's rays.

'Amazing isn't it, Mike?' said Buddy from behind. 'You take off from somewhere in Florida, get up to space in less than ten minutes, make a few adjustments and you've suddenly found a tiny object in all this, travelling at crazy miles an hour around the earth.'

'Yeah,' was all Michael could say. They were now only sixty seconds from docking and he wanted to savour this moment. He and Buddy had been the first children on a spacecraft launch and after just four hours they were about to board the ISS.

Ralph switched the controls to manual and with Steve's assistance, manoeuvred *Inceptor 1* until it was perfectly lined up with the ISS.

Michael imagined that docking a spacecraft was like trying to insert a plug straight into a socket that was moving.

'And steady...hold it there, Steve,' said Ralph.

The crew capsule screen showed a black and white image of an inverted cone with a hole in the centre. Figures on the screen displayed the dimensions of the docking port and the distance from it. *Inceptor 1*'s probe needed to be inserted into the very centre.

'Approaching docking port. Reducing speed. One metre,' said Ralph, as if he was describing reversing into a car park space.

Michael swallowed and flexed his clammy hands. How could Ralph be so calm?

'Fifty centimetres...steady,' said Ralph, his eyes still fixed on the screen. 'Twenty...ten...five and...docking *Inceptor 1* to the ISS.'

Arms that looked like crab claws extended from the ISS and grabbed hold of *Inceptor 1*. The probe then retracted and the two vehicles were pulled together. The very slightest, dull clunk signalled the two crafts becoming one.

'Mission Control, this is *Inceptor 1*,' said Ralph. 'Docking procedure executed. The probe is secure. Contact and capture.'

Once the pressure between the ISS and *Inceptor 1* had

been equalised, boarding could begin.

'Hey, Mike. How do you organise a space party?' said Buddy suddenly from behind.

Michael screwed up his nose like he'd had a whiff of something hideous. He'd listened to a constant stream of Buddy's jokes during the last eighteen months of training and must have heard every single one of them at least twice by now.

'I don't know, Buddy, but I've got a suspicion you're going to tell me.'

'You planet...get it...plan it...Awesome, isn't it?' he said, slapping his legs and grinning.

Typical Buddy. Only he could talk rubbish at a time like this. Michael gave him a 'shut up' stare and noticed that his face was littered with frown lines.

Knock... Knock...

But this wasn't a 'knock, knock' joke. It was actual knocking coming from the other side of the hatch.

Marat pulled himself along the roof of the crew capsule. He rapped his knuckles on the white inside, creating a metal echo, like the lowest note on a steel drum.

Michael fiddled with his three-point harness, eventually releasing it. There was that bizarre feeling again as his body rose away from his seat and hovered.

'Mission Control, this is *Inceptor 1*,' said Ralph. 'Crew ready to disembark.'

Now the red arrow on the hatch door handle moved a hundred and eighty degrees in the opposite direction to four hours ago. Ralph pulled on the handle, breaking the suction seal and the door opened.

A head, with neatly cropped dark hair and a sad mouth, filled the opening. But once the head and body had turned the right way around, it was one of the Chinese crew, looking almost as excited as a four-year-old on Christmas morning.

'Greetings from the International Space Station to *Inceptor 1*. I am Ru Wang and this is the *Dàdǎn* commander, Shen Ye. We would like to extend our hospitality and welcome you on board,' he said, thrusting out a hand.

After gliding through the hatch like a diver, Marat was the first to introduce himself. Michael was really impressed that he could speak Chinese. He and Buddy had been learning Russian for two years now and although they could understand technical terms and spacecraft procedures, he wasn't sure that either of them could chat away like Marat.

Michael grabbed his helmet, gloves and manual and stuffed them into his flight bag. The only other things he'd brought were a picture of his family and the autograph book his dad had given him before he left the UK. Then he reached up for the object floating just above his head. 'Come on, Cyril. Time to go.'

Cyril, a red, white and blue stuffed alligator, was *Inceptor 1*'s mascot.

Sarah left the crew capsule next, followed by Steve, then Ralph.

'Hey, Mike. D'you mind if I go next? I've gotta get out of here,' said Buddy, already propelling himself towards the hatch opening.

They'd spent hundreds of hours working in a life-sized mock-up of the ISS in the Neutral Buoyancy Pool (NBP) at the Florida Space Center (FSC). In the world's largest pool they'd simulated weightlessness and practised for life in space but, right now, it was as if none of that had taken place. With his bag strapped on, Michael pulled himself along the roof of *Inceptor 1*, like a clumsy imitation of Spiderman. Even though moving was easy, stopping was tricky and he bumped into the roof, almost missing the open mouth of the hatch.

Once safely in the airlock, he followed the stream of chatter in front of him to the US *Destiny* module. The others were floating mid-air, chatting, as if it was the most natural thing to do. He looked around at the mass of switches, vents, buttons, levers and wires and recognised everything. He was so far away from home, yet this odd, metal cylinder felt reassuringly familiar.

'OK, guys. If I could have your attention please,' said Ralph, creating an instantaneous hush. 'Firstly, I want to say congratulations on a faultless flight here and a perfect docking manoeuvre. Secondly, I'd like to say a formal hello to our Chinese colleagues. I know it's been a long time coming but it's great that our countries have finally decided to play ball. We're looking forward to having dinner with you guys and sharing some downtime.'

Ru Wang and Shen Ye looked at each other and smiled, then nodded to each member of the *Inceptor 1* crew in turn.

'And finally,' said Ralph, turning towards Michael and Buddy, 'we must recognise the enormous achievement of these two guys here. At fifteen years old they were the best on the Children's Moon Program (CMP), so impressive that NASA decided to give them both the opportunity to fly on this mission. They've shown us a thing or two during training and they are, right now, the first children in space.'

Michael immediately felt that familiar burn in his cheeks. He'd always been like this and even though he'd done better at being in the limelight recently, he still hated it. He looked at Buddy for help, but he was turned away from the group, clutching his stomach. 'Er...thanks,' he said, willing his eyes up from the floor. 'Buddy and I seem to have been doing tests and simulations forever and although it's all I've ever wanted to do, I suppose we can't believe that we're actually here. Er...thanks for giving us this opportunity and I hope we do a good job for you.'

'Thanks, Michael,' said Ralph. 'OK then, before we get a chance to look around and get some food, we've got a couple of things to do. It's traditional that any new crew do the cooking and cleaning for the first week, so that'll be you guys,' he said, looking straight at Michael and Buddy.

Michael flashed a look at Buddy. Cooking and cleaning? If they saw his bedroom they wouldn't ask him to clean and if they'd tasted his excuse for a spaghetti bolognaise (or 'blobonaise' as his sister, Millie, called it), they definitely wouldn't allow him anywhere near the kitchen.

'Just joking, Michael,' said Ralph, bearing an expanse of perfect teeth. 'Now, we've got about ten minutes before Mission Control is going to hook us up to our families, which means I can brief you on some changes to our mission.

They hadn't even spoken to Mission Control and Ralph was making changes. What was all that about, thought Michael?

The start of the briefing was as expected. Ralph read out some of the press coverage on the *Fortis* mission. It would be the first mission in a US commercially-built spacecraft taking off from US soil. They'd be returning to the moon after a long absence, landing on the far side for the first time and the US would be the first nation to train a child to take on an astronaut role. Michael thought that bit made Buddy and him seem a bit like monkeys. He knew that Ralph had to talk about all this stuff, but he couldn't wait to get down to the mission detail.

But the atmosphere suddenly changed as Ralph explained the new scope of their mission.

'I don't understand,' said Buddy. 'I thought we'd agreed our timetable and mission objectives. I don't get what you've just said, Ralph.'

'I know this will come as a bit of a shock, but we couldn't risk telling you on the ground for security reasons. The new mission documents were only placed in *Inceptor 1* two hours before launch and they'll be destroyed before we return to earth.'

Chapter Two

'But isn't every experiment secret?' said Buddy, frowning. 'I mean, we only report things if we find anything major, don't we? The rest stays as research or we follow it up the next time someone's here?'

'Yes, you're right, Buddy,' said Ralph, flicking over one of the pages in the plastic folder he was holding. 'Normally that's exactly what we'd do, but this is no ordinary situation. I'll let you all have a good look through the document on this, so you understand the detail, but essentially what we're about to be involved in is potentially world-changing...in fact life-changing. You cannot speak to anyone else about this; not to family or friends online or even over the radio channel to Mission Control. The only conversations about it can be had here on the ISS and not during radio contact. Is that clear?'

The crew waited in turn for the red folder and scanned its typewritten pages. Sarah held the documents for longest, her eyebrows permanently high on her forehead as she read and re-read what was in front of her.

Then it was Michael's turn. The chemical symbols and names made no sense to him at all, so he flicked forwards to the expected findings on the final page. It read:

From previous lunar probe samples examined at the Florida Space Center, we can conclude that the addition of element XO3 to protein PM4, tested in an accelerated environment, such as microgravity, is likely to produce an effective vaccine against the abnormal division of cells, commonly known as cancer.

Michael re-read the last sentence over and over. The words 'vaccine against...cancer' kept jumping out at him from the page. He looked up at Ralph and the other crew, who all had the same look of incomprehension etched across their faces.

'So the research with PM4 last time…'

'Yes, Sarah, your research last time was groundbreaking,' interrupted Ralph. 'You managed to get the PM4 sample to reproduce massively faster here than on earth. What you didn't know is that the protein we call PM4 is the protein present when abnormal cells divide in the body. It's the sort of *driver*. It's what lies at the heart of all cancerous cells.'

Sarah rolled her eyes. 'OK, so we found out that PM4 is the protein at the heart of cancerous cells, but what's XO3 got to do with it and how do we know it can help?'

Michael was just about following the conversation but what exactly was this XO3 and how were they going to get hold of it?

'Two years ago, NASA sent a lunar explorer to the far side of the moon, as you know. *Venture* visited multiple sites, collecting samples. One of those samples contained what we now call XO3.

'But how come I didn't know anything about this as the mission specialist? I was the one working on the PM4 samples. Why wasn't I told?'

'The NASA Research Center thought it too big a deal to talk about at that stage. There were only three other people who knew about it and they were sworn to secrecy,' said Ralph, with a look that told Michael that he wasn't going to say who they were. 'They did initial tests, as they do with all new substances, and found that XO3 interferes with proteins. When they added enough of it to a PM4 sample that had been in microgravity, it stopped the abnormal division of cells; but we didn't have the volume of XO3 samples to prove it beyond all doubt.'

'And that's the real reason we're here?' said Sarah.

'Well, that and the first landing on the far side of the

moon,' said Ralph. 'And the first children to go into space,' he added, looking at Michael and Buddy.

Suddenly the whole mission felt fake...like they were just a cover story for the real news. Michael thought back to Bob Sturton's comments in training about '...identifying the moon's resources...' and '...key scientific research.' Had he known about this all along?

Steve shouted from behind: 'Is that why our mission was accelerated?'

'Partly, but there's something else I need to tell you,' said Ralph, looking even less comfortable than before. 'Yes, we're here five months earlier than planned, but that's for a different reason.'

'Look, I'm confused,' said Steve. 'What's this all about, Ralph and why weren't we briefed about it? We're the ones putting our lives on the line coming up here. We're the ones leaving our families and friends and spending sixteen hours a day working in a 'tin can'. We've crammed two years of training into eighteen months for this mission. How come you're changing the goal posts now we're up here?'

All eyes were fixed on Ralph, who was bobbing in front of them like a human helium balloon.

'The Chinese,' said Ralph, pointing to one end of the *Destiny* module.

'And...what about the Chinese?' asked Steve, his face now taking on a reddish hue.

'Firstly, NASA had absolutely no idea that the President would change his mind and welcome China as an ISS partner. You know as well as I do that he'd rejected the idea for years due to China's appalling human rights record.'

'...And secondly?' said Steve, quickly.

'...And secondly...'

Suddenly, from behind them, Ru appeared; 'Ah. Good

evening, *Fortis* crew.'

Michael swung around as quickly as microgravity would allow and twitched a quick, insincere smile.

'Um...good evening, Ru. It's good to see you again. What can we do for you?' said Ralph, snapping shut the folder.

'Well, I know you have much to discuss about your exciting mission but I wondered if you would allow your new Chinese partners to provide you with food this evening? Shen is in the galley preparing our first meal together. If you would like to come,' he said, pointing in the direction of the new Chinese *Dàdǎn* module.

'Can we follow you down in about fifteen minutes, Ru? We've got a link up with Mission Control shortly but then we'd love some food, thanks.'

In a hushed voice this time and checking that Ru had gone, Ralph continued. 'As soon as the Chinese government received the go-ahead that they'd been accepted as an ISS partner, they started building.'

Michael could see nothing odd about this.

'But they didn't take the usual number of flights over a few years to construct their module...they built it in three months.'

'What? That's extraordinary,' said Steve. 'Why would they do that? It must have cost a fortune.'

'Exactly, Steve.'

'Perhaps there was a private investor,' said Sarah. 'There must be millions of rich Chinese who might make a contribution in return for a future visit to the ISS?'

Ralph rubbed his chin and leaned in. 'We don't know how reliable our source is but we believe that the Chinese government research team is also working on a cancer vaccine.'

The crew fell silent. The only noise now was the

humming, banging and creaking of the ISS.

'And that's why our mission was brought forward? It's all because we can't bear to lose the race to find some medical vaccine. Are you serious?' said Sarah, bouncing up towards the ceiling.

'Sarah, I know this is a bit of a shock for you and you feel that you've been…'

'Lied to, Ralph, that's what I've been…lied to!'

'I know it seems tough, but sometimes these things aren't so simple…'

'Stop using someone else's political jargon, Ralph and be honest,' said Sarah, raising her voice.

This was all getting very uncomfortable and Michael had no idea what to do or say.

'We have information to suggest that the Chinese have been working on a vaccine for years. Clearly, they won't get to the moon for a while but maybe XO3 isn't the only substance that can destroy the PM4 protein,' said Ralph, 'which would mean that we've spent millions of dollars and years of research for nothing.'

'So we just change our research plans, prove it works, release our own vaccine and save millions of lives across the world,' hissed Sarah.

'If I can just interject,' said Steve, holding his palms out like a double stop sign. 'I think what Ralph may be getting at, is that the US want to be the first to market with this vaccine and that we have a chance to start the ball rolling on this mission.'

'You mean the US government want to be first out with a vaccine and then sell it to the rest of the world before the Chinese get there?' said Sarah.

'Well…'

'What you're saying is that it's about rushing a vaccine to market so that we can benefit most. It's about money and has anyone even thought about whether it's fair to involve two teenagers in this? Are you really planning to ask Michael to collect this XO3 on his moon mission?' Sarah shook her head, pushed herself off towards the end of the module and disappeared.

Another silence. Michael looked at the floor. What could he say to make the atmosphere better? He glanced at Buddy, who shrugged.

Then Marat, who'd been silent since arriving on the ISS, spoke. 'I think it is important to stay calm here,' he said, in a heavily accented voice. 'I see no problem with us completing our research and returning home with the results. If we have something ready to go to market, then the US will go to market. I do not think we need to concern ourselves with what the Chinese may or may not be doing.'

'Well put, Marat,' said Ralph. 'I know this is tough and I understand Sarah's frustration. When we've spoken to Mission Control and everyone's calmed down a bit, there's something I can share with you that should make the mission changes a little more meaningful, but I've got to ask you to keep it to yourselves.'

Before anyone could speak, Ralph left to get Sarah and within a few minutes, it was time to face the world.

'This will be streamed live on air,' said Ralph, 'so I don't need to tell you guys to keep it brief. Sarah, I don't want you getting all lovey-dovey with your husband, or getting tearful when you have to say goodbye. Steve, you can ask a quick question about your Tottenham Hot-whatever soccer team, but don't go asking for a full match analysis. You can do that when you're on your own later. Understood?'

Everyone nodded.

It was a challenge to all get in the same place at the same time, much to Michael's frustration. Every time he got himself in front of Sarah or Steve, he'd start drifting off in another direction. Then, when he thought he'd corrected himself, he went too far the other way.

Ralph smiled, allowing it to happen a few times, before grabbing his t-shirt and pulling him down towards the floor. 'There's a strap down there, Michael,' he said, pointing to a loop of white nylon. 'Just stick one foot through that and you'll stay put. If not, we can always get a giant piece of Velcro and use that.'

With a bit of manoeuvring and grabbing each other and after Sarah had stopped the crew from laughing at her by tying back her hair, they were ready.

'Mission Control, this is Ralph Grant and the crew from *Inceptor 1* on board the ISS. Good afternoon.'

The screen immediately awoke with a perfect picture. At least two members of each family lined up on comfy couches, looking almost as awkward as Michael felt. The only exception was Marat. He'd mumbled something about his mother not wanting to see him 'up there again' and sat at the back of the group looking like he'd rather be anywhere else. Michael took a deep breath and tried to make the corners of his mouth face upwards.

His granny was in her favourite lilac colours, wearing the lucky pearls that Michael's grandpa had given her. She always wore them on special occasions. Next to his granny sat his parents, Tim and Viv and on the end of one couch was his sister, Millie. He'd always found her the most annoying person in the world, but since he'd got his place on the *Fortis* mission, he had to admit, she'd been a brilliant little sister. She'd even stayed out of his bedroom.

Michael scanned the screen quickly to try and work out who belonged to whom but was interrupted by John Dell.

'Good afternoon, International Space Station. This is John Dell at Mission Control with Bob Sturton and Jamie Matheson...and a few others you may recognise.'

Everyone on the couches waved and instinctively the crew did the same.

'You are live on air across the world, so can we please remind you to watch what you say.'

'Hello to the crew of *Inceptor 1*,' said a bald-headed man, with a military-style about him. 'This is Bob Sturton, Head of Training at NASA. Well done on your seamless launch and successful docking at the ISS. I think everyone here would like to know how you're all feeling now you're up there?'

There was a pause and Michael wondered if he should say something. Seeing Bob's face was great. He ran the Children's Moon Program (CMP) and was their lead trainer for this mission, but how did he feel now that he was two hundred and forty miles above the people he was looking at?

'Hi there,' said Sarah, smiling and waving slowly. 'We're doing great, thanks. Everything went according to plan. We're excited to be here and can't wait to get on with our mission. It's a short one this time for some of us, so we're keen to get started.' Sarah kept her smile for as long as she could before it collapsed into a wobbly line. 'I love you, honey. Look after Snoopy for me.'

'Hi, this is Steve Winters. I want to say a big hello to everyone in the UK. I'm proud to have been the pilot today and with Ralph's expertise, it was a textbook journey here. I'm really looking forward to getting on with the mission.'

Each crewmember took turns at speaking, first about the mission and then to their families. Soon there was only Buddy and Michael left.

By now Buddy's face had a funny sheen to it and he was still hunched over as if he'd been punched in the stomach. 'Hi, this is Buddy Russell. I'm honoured to have been selected for the *Fortis* mission and I'm really looking forward to working as the mission specialist support with Sarah Hutchins. Mom, I love you and miss you already. I won't be able to take a shower but I promise I'll clean my teeth twice a day.'

He's feeling ill and still, he's better at doing this than me, thought Michael, trying to get what he wanted to say straight in his head. 'Er...hello. This is Michael May and I'm really happy to be on the *Fortis* mission, working with all of these experienced and talented astronauts. Er...I'm really looking forward to my time on board the ISS and our exciting journey to the moon. Actually, it seems unreal just saying those words...and very...er...special. Mum, Dad, Millie and Granny...thank you for supporting me in following my dreams and please try not to do your worrying thing. I will be OK and I'll be in touch properly later.'

Before ending the hook-up, Ralph answered a couple of questions about their activities over the next two days. There were also a few words from Jamie Matheson about his job as Flight Activities Officer at Mission Control. He was in charge of checking space station software, preparing timetables for the crew each day and logging any data they sent down to Mission Control. He finished with a quick message to Michael and Buddy.

'Now guys, I know you're only up there because I bombed out right at the end of the CMP but you've got to make the most of it. If you need a chat anytime, just give me a call and if I'm not out skateboarding, I'll be here for you,' he said, grinning. 'Oh, and I'll be sending you your work schedules later, so you'd better get your heads down and get on with it.'

Michael returned Jamie's smile without thinking about the millions of people watching. He'd become really good friends with Buddy and Jamie and couldn't believe how well they'd done, considering what'd been going on at home. Buddy's dad had left four years earlier, causing his mum's eating to spiral out of control ever since. It worried him like mad, but there wasn't much he could do to help. For Jamie, things had been even worse. His mum had been ill for nearly three years. Michael knew that part of him was glad that he'd not made it onto the mission. He was still involved but close by if his mum needed him. It made Michael's worries about fitting into school in Florida and leaving everything and everyone behind in Andoverford seem pathetic.

The crew got to say their last goodbyes. There were a few shout-outs from their families back in Florida and Sarah cried again when her husband said he loved her.

Ralph turned off the monitor and there was silence.

Was everyone else thinking the same thing, thought Michael? Were they suddenly realising how far away and how alone they were up in this alien 'space creature' of wires, shapes and engines? Were they worried about three fifteen-year-olds being part of such a crucial mission? And what about the rest of Ralph's briefing? What else was he going to tell them?

Chapter Three

'Right, guys,' said Ralph, clapping his hands. 'Once we've accepted the hospitality of our new ISS partners, I'll finish the briefing and you can get acquainted with your temporary home.'

'Um, Ralph. I think we're going to have to wait a few minutes before we head off,' said Steve, flicking his head up and towards the end of the *Destiny* module. 'I think Buddy's starting to feel the effects of microgravity,' he said, jabbing his index finger towards his open mouth.

'What do we do?' asked Michael. His stomach almost revolted at the thought.

'Not a lot we can do, Michael,' said Sarah, pulling herself away in Buddy's direction. 'You've just got to deal with it until it goes away. I just want to make sure that he's OK and can find everything he needs. I wouldn't want anything nasty escaping and floating around.'

Poor Buddy, thought Michael. That's why he'd wanted to get out of *Inceptor 1* so quickly.

It was nearly twenty minutes before Sarah returned with a wax-faced Buddy.

'You OK?' asked Michael, not wanting to get too close in case he smelt it.

'Yeah.' Buddy nodded.

'He just needs to wait a while and then have some fluids,' said Sarah, rubbing Buddy's back. 'Once he's eaten we'll give him some medication to help with nausea.'

'Then let us go and see what the Chinese team have done with their new module,' said Marat, pushing himself off one of the walls. 'I hear they have some state of the art equipment.'

Michael's attempt to follow Marat wasn't entirely

successful. He obviously pushed off too hard and ended up banging straight up and into what would normally be the roof. He heard a snort behind him.

'Come on then, Buddy, if you're so good at this!' said Michael, swinging round in the corridor. There wasn't a lot of room to move, particularly in one of these storage modules, with rows of drawers, bundles of clothes and boxes of equipment. He glided past air vents and filters and many of the corridors had lengths of wiring clipped to the sides. It reminded him of the chaos in his bedroom.

As he pretended to fly, Michael peered into more portholes and hatches feeding off the main corridors. He'd memorised the whole layout of the ISS. He'd walked and swam through big sections of it in training, but this was different. Now he was here, he could get a much better sense of the sheer size of this thing. With more room than his own house and larger in expanse than the football pitch he used to play on back in England, it was vast. Yet the mass of tiny spaces, cramped areas and cubbyholes made if feel far smaller.

When he reached the Chinese galley Michael managed to manoeuvre himself alongside the nearest thing they had to a table, without crashing into it. It had shallow, rectangular holes, strips of Velcro around the edges and reminded him of the Lego stations in shops, designed to keep children quiet whilst their parents shopped.

'Thanks a lot for inviting us to dinner,' said Ralph, as Ru took several silver pouches with yellow tabs on them out of a tiny oven and deposited them in the Lego holes. 'And congratulations on being the first Chinese mission to the ISS. You must be very excited.'

Ru nodded. 'It has taken many years to persuade your country that we will be beneficial partners, but we are really happy to be here and have some important work to carry out. Now let us eat and get to know one another properly.'

Michael picked up the pouch in front of him. The label displayed a line of Chinese characters.

'It is our special Chinese pork and rice and is really tasty – better than the American food,' said Ru.

Michael twisted the short tube at the top of the pouch and brought it up to his mouth. He got a waft of something like the barbeque sauce glaze he loved on American ribs. He couldn't wait to try out the menus that the NASA dieticians had selected for him, but the best bit was going to be the special treat that each astronaut had ordered. Steve had gone for a few bars of his favourite chocolate, as had Marat. Sarah had asked for apple pie to remind her of home and Ralph wanted peanut butter. Michael had thought very carefully about what to choose. Should it be sweet or savoury? Should it be a drink or something to eat? Buddy was bringing salt and vinegar crisps, but they took up so much room that he'd been limited to just a few packets. In the end, after a lot of deliberating, he went for caramel cookies. He'd discovered these amazing, crispy-yet-gooey cookies when he'd moved to Florida and could easily put a whole packet away in one sitting.

The Chinese pork tasted heavenly. The only downside was that it had to be chopped up small enough to be squeezed through the pouch tube, so it didn't quite feel like a proper meal.

Dessert was a surprise. As soon as he twisted the end of the tube, he got a whiff of fruit and vanilla. The combination of stewed pear with vanilla cream tasted amazing and Michael could have wolfed down another two or three.

The conversation around the table was formal, to begin with. Michael tried to find questions to ask the Chinese crew, but he couldn't get what Ralph had said out of his head. Did Ru and Shen know about XO3? Were they also here to work on a vaccine for cancer?

'How are you finding it here so far?' Michael asked Shen.

'Yes, very agreeable,' said Shen, quickly. 'We are enjoying our first time at the International Space Station very much.'

'We were told that there were three of you coming up to the ISS?' said Steve, finishing a mouthful of dessert.

'Oh...yes...there are three of us but, like your colleague Buddy, our third crew member, Yue Shi, has been suffering from dreadful space sickness and is confined to her sleep station. We are hoping that she will join us tomorrow when we start our most important work,' said Ru.

'And what's that?' asked Ralph.

'Well, we have many experiments to perform,' said Ru, clearing the table and handing round pouches of drinks. 'We are researching how the immune system is compromised by microgravity and how we can prevent calcium from disappearing from bones. It follows on from some of the research that NASA has already done in this area.'

'D'you think you're close to any meaningful answers?' asked Sarah.

'We are not as close to an answer as we would like to be. We are going to be doing some tests on Shen now we have been here for a month and see if we can identify the trigger to cell changes. Perhaps we should have a conversation about this one evening, Sarah?'

'Yeah, sure. Sounds interesting.'

'And we are very excited to hear about your far side mission. This is something China is also aiming to do soon. What are you expecting to find?' Ru looked straight at Michael.

This was the question he'd been dreading. What should he say? He hoped his stupid face didn't give the game away, but he could feel the heat creeping up his cheeks already.

'Perhaps I can answer that for you,' said Ralph, using his charming, broad smile. 'We need to survey the general geography of the area. Apart from remote images, we don't have a lot of data about the far side. Then we'll do what we did on the moon last time...we'll take some samples for analysis and see what we find. We're looking for water-rich samples. You're welcome to come to the *Destiny* lab sometime to see what we're doing.'

What? Michael didn't get it. Why would Ralph say that? What was he playing at?

The meal finished with a conversation about the spacewalks (Extra Vehicular Activities – or EVAs for short) that each crew would be carrying out. Ralph and Marat would be setting up an experiment on top of the *Destiny* module before carrying out some repairs on the underside of the *Harmony* node, whilst Ru and Shen were going to be finishing the construction of an airlock and hatch on the *Dàdǎn* module.

Michael's thoughts flashed forward to his spacewalk; not just outside the ISS, but on the moon. Already so far away from everything he knew, in just three days' time, he'd have to go another thousand times further into space. Not only that, there was the added complexity of landing on the far side for the first time and the pressure of having to bring back their secret samples.

After enthusiastic goodbyes from Ru and Shen, Buddy whispered to Michael. 'Let's go back to *Destiny* via the *Cupola*, Mike. I can't wait 'til later and if we're quick, it won't take long.'

Michael nodded and they shot off like torpedoes.

'Hey, Mike. Just imagine if Jia Li hadn't been found out and had made it onto this mission instead of me. You'd be doing this with her.'

Michael screwed up his nose. This was exactly the kind of thing he didn't want to imagine. That lying, cheating girl had deliberately sabotaged three of the other candidates on the CMP to give herself a better chance of winning. She'd also locked him in a cupboard and tried to drown him. He was just glad she'd been found out and kicked off the programme. He couldn't think of a better result than having Buddy here and Jamie at Mission Control.

The *Cupola* reminded Michael of the ball turret on a B17 Flying Fortress bomber. His favourite war film showed the brave gunner climbing into a glass ball on the plane's belly, ready to pick off the enemy, but a sitting target himself.

On the ISS, the *Cupola* was a European Space Agency-built observatory module. It had a round window at the bottom surrounded by six other windows, making up a hexagon. Astronauts would come here to complete earth observations, experiments or to gaze at the unique views below.

Right now, as Michael and Buddy looked beneath them, they could see hair-like wisps of cloud combed across changing shapes. It took them a few moments to work it out, but there was soon no mistaking the familiar shape of the African continent.

'Isn't that just the most awesome thing you've ever seen?' said Buddy, pulling himself round to see out of the other windows. 'I've never been to Africa before. My mom would just love it.'

Michael laughed. 'After seeing your mum's face on the Mission: SPACE ride I'm not sure you'd get her up here, let alone get her to look down. D'you remember what she was like when you were about to get on the g-force simulator at the Florida Space Center?'

'That's true. Second thoughts…she'd hate it, Mike. Best leave all this to us experts, hey.'

As Michael watched the earth's swirling colours race by, the word *expert* couldn't be further from how he felt.

As well as the best view known to man, the *Cupola* also housed two hand controllers that operated a super-sized, multi-jointed robotic arm called the SSRMS (Space Station Remote Manipulator System). It looked like something straight out of a fantasy movie. Seven motorised sections allowed this spindly, metal arm to reach out seventeen metres. Operating it felt like controlling someone's shoulder, elbow, wrist and fingers all at the same time.

Callie Granger, the NASA robotics expert, had spent months teaching the boys how to use the hand controllers and switches. When they'd made a mistake, it had been back to the start until they got it right. They couldn't afford to mess up when they were moving payloads, equipment and people around two hundred and forty miles above the earth.

By the time Michael and Buddy got back to the *Destiny* module, the others had already unpacked and were busy checking the computer systems and equipment around them.

'Right, guys,' said Ralph at one screen. 'Jamie's sent through a protocol of checks we need to do before we get our first night's sleep in our new home and we've also got our timetables for the next two weeks. I've stuck a set on the wall for you, next to your screen. Just run the checks and mark as complete when you're done.'

Michael pulled his checklist from the Velcro and scanned it.

'I've got temperature and humidity controls. What've

you got?' asked Buddy, flicking over his sheets of paper and cross-checking with his screen.

'Er…contamination and carbon dioxide removal,' said Michael, wishing Buddy would be quiet for once.

'Sorry. Looks like you've got a problem on your hands then.'

'What?' said Michael, checking the screen again for something he might have missed.

'I mean, the launch, the sickness and those pills…I can tell you there's going to be some serious air contamination in my sleep station tonight, dude,' laughed Buddy, patting his stomach.

'Very funny. Can I get on in peace now please?' Michael ran through every line on his spreadsheet, checking the readings and measurements and logging them. His job was to make sure there wasn't anything harmful in the air.

His second check was on the carbon dioxide removal assemblies. These machines allowed for the safe removal of the carbon dioxide produced by nine astronauts. All his figures fell within the normal parameters.

Next, Michael looked at the rest of his schedule. He thought his school timetable, combined with his mission-training schedule had been detailed until he saw this. Every fifteen minutes had been allocated to a colour-coded activity. Blue was sleep. He'd been allotted eight hours but not always at the same time of the night. If he was involved in one of the experiments, he'd probably be later. If not, he'd be earlier. Red was for experiments. Now he knew what the real plan was and what was at stake, he didn't even know if they'd be doing any of their original research on plants, bone density and respiratory illnesses. Yellow was mealtime, purple was exercise and green was leisure time. He couldn't wait to video call his family and was already dying to go back to the *Cupola*.

'How's it going, Michael?' asked Sarah as she came alongside him.

She looked far less weird since she'd tamed her blond hair with one of those stretchy things his sister, Millie, wore. She also reminded him of his mum – confident, sometimes a little overbearing, but with a good heart.

'I'm fine, thanks,' answered Michael, re-attaching his checklist to the wall. 'I guess I'm just a bit worried about what Ralph said earlier. It changes everything, doesn't it?'

Sarah nodded. 'Try not to worry, Michael. It's quite common for NASA to change things around at the last minute. There's nothing we can do. We've just got to get on and trust that they've made the right call.'

Try not to worry. He hadn't been able to think of much else.

Once the *Fortis* crew had carried out their checks, Ralph called them together. 'Tomorrow marks the start of our real work,' he said. 'I know our mission goals have changed, but I want you all to approach it positively. Whatever we do here is for the common good and I don't want you to lose sight of that.' He paused and clenched his jaw. 'But this mission also has a personal angle to it, which might give you a different perspective.'

Michael looked at Buddy, who shrugged.

'The PM4 samples we've brought with us aren't just nameless samples from some research laboratory. Both the patient and NASA's lead science director have given their consent. The samples are from someone we all know.'

Chapter Four

'It's Jamie's mum, isn't it?' Michael said, answering everyone's question. 'She's just had her last round of chemotherapy. Jamie told me and Buddy that if it doesn't work, there's not a lot more they can do for her.'

'Yes, that's right, Michael. Obviously, we've known Liz for quite a while now but when Jamie saw the scope of the experiment, he asked us if we'd consider it.'

Poor Jamie thought Michael. Everyone had been so caught up in the excitement of the launch build-up that he hadn't even asked how his mum was. And the jokey Jamie they'd seen on the screen earlier had all this stuff going on in his head.

'Who else knows?' asked Steve.

'Just the research team, Jamie, John and Bob,' answered Ralph.

'So this just got a whole lot more important,' said Buddy, pushing back his gelled, black hair. 'Forget getting a vaccine to market, we've got to hope it works for Jamie's mom.'

The *Destiny* module fell silent before Ralph spoke. 'Take some time to absorb all this and we'll talk again tomorrow.'

Michael didn't know if it was the excitement of launch, the long day or the overload of information, but sleep started to lean heavily on his eyelids. He made his way to the toilet cubicle and slid across the white plastic curtain. How did Ralph or Marat manage to move around in this thing?

When he peered in the mirror it reflected a stranger's face. His mop of curly brown hair now framed a red and puffy face.

Buddy already had his curtain pulled across by the time

he got back to the sleep stations. So did Steve and Sarah. Michael had chosen what they called 'the room in the roof'. He had to turn upside down into a handstand and push himself up into his little area of privacy. This would be it for the next eight weeks: the only room here that was his.

In this tiny haven, Michael changed for bed and set his clock. The ISS operated on London Greenwich Mean Time (GMT) as it was halfway between Russian and US time, so it was now three o'clock in the morning for him.

Despite his body begging for sleep, he needed to call home. He clicked the 'live chat' button on his laptop and waited. A few seconds later, his mum and dad's excitable faces covered the entire screen. Michael's shoulders relaxed.

'Hi, Michael. How are you doing, Son?' asked his dad, with his usual grin. 'How was your launch? Is that your sleep station? Have you had one of those reconstituted meals I read about – maybe rum and raisin ice-cream?'

'Whoa! Steady on, Dad. What's with all the questions? Give me a chance.'

Michael's mum was already nudging her husband in the ribs as he was talking. 'Tim, just let the poor boy answer the first question. It's not a race.' She smiled a big, comforting, I'm-worried-about-you-but-not-going-to-show-it smile, which Michael tried to return.

'I like your hair, Mum. It suits you,' he said quickly, making everything momentarily normal. 'Nice shirt, Dad but you've got ketchup down your chin again.' Michael laughed as his dad stretched over to look at the small picture of himself in the corner of the screen. 'Gotcha!'

'So how's it going, Michael? How was the launch?'

'I bet it was a lot more spectacular for you than it was for us, crammed into the crew capsule.'

His dad was nodding, desperate to talk.

'You remember when we went on those rides at the Disney parks, Dad? The Mission: SPACE ride, where you vomited and Space Mountain, where you lost your bet about holding on?' said Michael, grinning. 'Well, this was like both of those put together, multiplied by a thousand. You'd have died, Dad. The g-force was amazing.'

'Millie's in bed but she says to tell you that her friends think you're the coolest person around and can you email them to say hi if she sends you their addresses?' said his mum, shrugging. 'You know Millie.'

'Say hi from me...actually, I'm going to have to go now,' he said, failing to suppress a yawn. 'They only give us eight hours sleep here and you know what I'm like in the mornings. I'll call again soon. Can you give Granny May a hug when you see her and give her that website so she can spot the ISS please?'

'Of course, Michael,' said his mum. 'We'll let you get some rest. Everyone's so proud of you. Carlie Russell asked us to say thanks for looking after Buddy and Jamie says you're a hero.'

After two or three goodbyes, Michael logged out and switched off his laptop. If only he could talk to his parents properly and tell them what this mission was really about. He wriggled his way into his sleeping bag, like the reverse shedding of a snake's skin. He must look like some sort of weird football mascot, hands poking through slits in the sleeping bag and head partially covered by a hood of the same material. And which way did he sleep? Did it matter? By now he really had no sense of up or down but the decision was made for him by the sleep that curled over him like a black, starry wave.

Michael was in the middle of a space chase with three of his childhood superheroes and several Star Wars characters.

He'd been on the verge of catching the evil cosmonaut who'd stolen the secret of the universe, when the beep from his alarm clock woke him.

For a few seconds, he thought he'd jumped straight into an even stranger dream, where he'd been kidnapped into an alien world, tied up and locked in a cupboard. Then he realised where he was.

To get his bearings he looked for the row of photographs on his wall. Then he pushed himself around one hundred and eighty degrees and stared at the line-up. His family were gathered around the pool at their Florida home. Apart from his training, the weather and the pool were probably the coolest things about moving to the US. He'd even come to enjoy swimming again after all these years of hating it. Next to this was a photo of his girlfriend, Charlotte. Even though they'd only started going out together a few months before he'd moved to Florida, he could still talk to her about all sorts of stuff. He'd email her later.

'Morning, sleepy,' said Buddy, when Michael got to the galley. 'How were your first 140,000 miles in space?'

Michael rubbed his sticky, sore eyes. 'What?'

'140,000 miles. That's how far we've travelled whilst we've been sleeping. Cool, isn't it? That's 5.3 times around the world,' said Buddy, chewing.

'You're feeling better then?' said Michael, selecting his breakfast from one of the food racks and joining him at the table.

'I had a good clear-out again this morning and the tablets seem to be working, so I thought I'd try and eat something.'

'Oh great! I'd better wait to use the toilet then,' said Michael, shaking his head. 'The smell yesterday was deadly.'

'I do my best, Mike. I do my best.'

Eating in space involved sucking food out of a pouch, adding water to it or spreading it on something else, making the choice of food a bit restrictive. But Buddy seemed to have found an ingenious solution. 'Hey, catch this, Mike,' he said, pulling a tortilla wrap out of a packet, smearing it with chocolate spread and throwing it like a bread Frisbee.

Michael dived to his right, caught the tortilla and then spun it back towards Buddy, who flipped it on its side and returned it like an electric saw blade.

'Looks like you guys are enjoying your first morning on the ISS,' said Ralph, bringing his breakfast to the table. 'You've just missed the most spectacular sunrise as we flew over China.'

'Mm,' said Buddy, his mouth full of chocolate spread. 'I'm not so bothered about that, Ralph. The beauty of being up here is that we get to see another one in ninety minutes. Were you down in the *Cupola*?'

'Yeah. I just gave the SSRMS a quick check before we go out there today. Are you guys happy with what you're doing?'

Michael and Buddy nodded, cheeks bulging. Being part of a spacewalk was one of the things Michael was looking forward to most.

Ralph looked at his watch. 'You've got to check in with Sarah to adjust your experiment schedule, Buddy. Michael, you've got your contamination and CO2 checks. See you both at eleven thirty.'

'Ralph, before you go, can I ask you something about our moon mission,' said Michael. 'D'you think we're doing the right thing?'

Ralph smiled and patted Michael on the shoulder like his dad would. 'I'm not sure we're here to consider whether what we're doing is right or not, Michael. There are so many experiments we could be doing to help everyone on earth and who's to judge which is the most important. We've invented so many useful, life-enhancing products up here but I'd probably swap most of them for what we're doing this time. We could make a real, immediate difference to millions of lives. I say we give it all we've got and just picture Liz Matheson if we ever feel it's too difficult.'

The airlock resembled a spacesuit wardrobe. Four suits had been propped against the sides with protective cloth hoods covering the helmets. But these were much more than spacesuits. Called EMUs (Extravehicular Mobility Units) they acted as individual spacecraft for the astronauts, containing everything they needed to survive outside the ISS.

'Right, guys. This is where the fun begins,' said Ralph, taking off his trousers to reveal his *Maximum Absorbency Garment* (space nappy or diaper).

'I like your style, Ralph,' said Buddy, grinning and passing him the next item. Tubes filled with water snaked their way around a liquid cooling suit. Ralph could increase or decrease the temperature of the water to regulate his body heat. Next came the pressure suit, necessary for keeping body fluids in a liquid state and several layers later came the final thermal micrometeoroid layer. This was designed to reflect the sun's rays and stop tiny bits of space debris breaching the suit.

'People always wonder why astronauts look so clumsy,' said Buddy, passing Marat his gloves. 'If they could see that lot, they'd soon get it.'

Next were the primary life support systems. These contained oxygen for up to eight hours, a carbon dioxide removal system, as well as batteries and a radio. There was also water for pumping round their cooling suits and for drinking.

'Steve's on his way down to operate the airlock,' said Buddy, holding up his thumb. 'We're going to head off to the *Cupola* now and you'll hear from us in a few minutes. Good luck, guys and enjoy the view.'

Michael stared through the round window at the bottom of the *Cupola*. The word 'pitch black' wasn't even close. There were no visible stars, no moon, no light of any sort and it would soon be his turn to head off into it.

Buddy checked the three screens in front of him, which showed a black and white image of this monster limb from different angles. He pressed the startup buttons and pulled back the hand controller in front of him. The last piece of the robotic arm moved. This was the end effector – the robot version of a hand. Buddy manoeuvred it to one of the side rails and closed the hand around it.

'Great. Let's check the extension and then we're good to go,' said Buddy.

Michael took the arm control unit, opened the end effector and moved the controller forwards. The seventeen metres of white, skinny arm moved away from the ISS out into the darkness before Michael pulled it back in.

'Looks good to me, Mike.'

The boys performed the rest of their checks before radioing down to Ralph and Marat.

'We're good to go in the *Cupola*,' said Buddy.

A pump hummed as it reduced the pressure in the airlock. As soon as it stopped the spacewalk began.

Wearing more than 130kg of clothing and equipment would be impossible on earth but, in microgravity, Ralph and Marat were able to inch forwards.

Ralph turned a lever, released the payload bay hatch and pushed it into the blackness.

'Crew are extravehicular,' said Buddy, suddenly seeing two white shapes appear on one of his screens. 'Good morning to you, Ralph and Marat. This is Buddy Russell speaking from the *Cupola*. Just to let you know that we're ready and coming in for tethering.'

Michael was impressed. Despite Buddy's habit of messing about and not taking anything seriously, he was actually really good. He waited for the OK to come from Ralph before moving the robotic arm. Using his cameras, he had to move it out of sight and around the ISS until he reached his colleagues. He then used a combination of grapple fixtures and tethers to secure Ralph and Marat to the arm.

'Careful now, Michael,' said Ralph over the speaker. 'I know you guys practised whizzing this thing around in training and I was really impressed. But you've got live cargo on the end this time, so I'd appreciate a gentle ride please.'

Michael smiled, gently pushing the right controller forwards and moving the left controller to the right. It was just like they'd practised way back on the CMP, just on a much bigger scale and with two white, wriggly things called astronauts on the end.

He brought Ralph and Marat to the top of the *Destiny* module where Sarah wanted them to deposit four trays of human stem cells. The trays would remain there for several weeks, to measure the effects of intense radiation. Marat secured the trays to one of the struts crossing the *Destiny* module, before signalling that they were finished.

Next, they had to move to the *Harmony* node. Something had caused a power failure in a section of the ISS the day before, which meant that one of the electrical supply boxes had either short-circuited or been hit by a piece of debris. They'd switched to temporary auxiliary power, but Ralph and Marat had to find out the cause of the problem and get full power back to the ISS.

Buddy took charge for the next manoeuvre, carefully transporting Ralph and Marat to the belly of the *Harmony* node. There he inched them up towards the problem. 'Looks like something's blown to me,' said Buddy, moving as close to the screen as he could. 'See that bit there,' he said, trying to put his nose on it whilst his hands moved, 'it doesn't look right and there are wires poking out from the casing. It's either a strike from something whizzing past or it's been on fire.'

After fierce sun for the last half an hour, the light now faded rapidly. The boys had to rely on lights from the ISS's video cameras and those, which moved like insect antennae, on the astronauts' helmets.

'I can see the problem,' said Ralph, his voice straining with the effort of moving in his suit. 'Looks like the circuit has blown but, judging by the lack of cover on the unit, I'd say something's hit it. I think we can fix it, but it's a fiddly job. I wish I could take these gloves off. Marat, can you pass me the resource box, please.'

Michael watched Marat unclip one of the tethers on his belt and re-clip it to one of the rails near the electrical supply box. He then removed the second tether, enabling him to adjust his position and open up the box.

Even the tools had their own double tethers. The screwdriver Ralph picked up had to be attached to his belt before it could be untethered from the box. This made everything painfully slow, but the risk of equipment being lost out there was far worse.

Ralph used his pliers to remove the debris before Marat passed him replacement lengths of wire to screw back into place.

'We should be done soon,' said Buddy, 'then we can get on with our new experiment.'

Michael immediately had that spinning sensation in

his stomach again. 'What d'you think about all that stuff, Buddy? It makes me really nervous...you know the secrecy and all that.'

'I think it's awesome,' said Buddy, with his usual wicked smile. 'We could be involved in the most top-secret experiment for years and help out Jamie. Imagine what our friends are going to say when we can eventually tell them. If Sarah's experiment and your moon samples give us the answer we're looking for, we'll be heroes.'

How did Buddy do it? He didn't seem to be afraid of anything and looked at life as one big adventure. If only he could be like that.

'Last part of the repair now,' said Ralph. 'We'll give you the OK when we're clear and then you can turn the power back on to test the circuit.'

'Do you want me to take over and finish off?' asked Marat. 'It must be hard on your hands.'

'Yeah, I'd forgotten what it's like out here but I'm good, thanks.'

Ralph leaned in to reattach the last two lengths of wire. As he did a brilliant, white flash streaked across the screen.

'What was that?' said Buddy.

'Oh my...look!' said, Michael, pressing his hand against his mouth.

'Where?'

'There...on the right of the screen. It's Ralph!' Michael pointed to something that resembled one of the empty spacesuits in the airlock – unmoving and lifeless. 'Ralph's been blown off the node.'

'But that's impossible,' said Buddy, checking the three screens in turn. 'There was no power.'

'Well, something was strong enough to throw him off... and he's...'

'Not moving.'

Chapter Five

Seeing Ralph's limp body transported Michael right back to the CMP when Jia Li had deliberately hooked Aiko's oxygen tube around the ladder in the Neutral Buoyancy Pool. By the time he'd reached her, she was floating like a white plastic bag in the sea. Those had probably been the worst moments of his life. How could Jia Li have done something like that? Just the thought of it made his hands lock rigidly around the controllers.

'Mike, what are you doing? Mike, say something!' Buddy shook Michael's shoulder.

'Er...sorry. Er...let's call Steve and see what Marat can do to help. We've got to move Ralph back towards him first.' Michael grabbed the two controllers and pushed the right one downwards.

Ralph started to move but suddenly jerked in the opposite direction and away from Marat's outstretched arms.

'What are you doing?'

'It's...there's something wrong with the controllers,' said Michael, looking at his hands. 'I can't move them... no, they're moving by themselves...look.'

Buddy and Michael stared at the image of the robotic arm. It was moving Ralph up and away from Marat, who was still tethered to one of the rails.

'Steve, we've got a major problem down here,' radioed Michael. 'It looks like Ralph's just got an electric shock from another blowout and the controllers are malfunctioning. I can't bring him back in.'

Steve didn't reply and Michael couldn't wait. There must be something he could do. 'Marat,' he said quickly. 'What's happening out there? How's Ralph?'

Marat's slow and purposeful voice came back a few seconds later. 'I do not know what happened. Ralph put the last wires in place to screw down and there was a white flash. I think he is unconscious but I cannot reach him to check.'

'What else can I do, Marat? I think Steve's on his way down but the SSRMS is going mad. It's moving all over the place all by itself,' said Michael, the panic rising in him along with his breakfast.

'I will try to get as close to Ralph as I can but you are going to have to move him towards me,' said Marat, beginning to slide his tether along the rail on the side of the ISS.

'Ralph? Can you hear me, Ralph? This is Steve. It looks like there was some sort of power surge in the box you were repairing.'

There was silence.

'He's breathing,' Steve said, pointing to a read-out of the computer on Ralph's spacesuit.

Yes, the read-out showed that Ralph's oxygen levels were falling and carbon dioxide was being removed, which meant he was alive. Michael looked at Buddy, who was still completely transfixed by the horror outside.

Steve tried the hand controllers for the robotic arm but couldn't get them to cooperate either. 'I don't understand this. There's power to the robotic workstation and the joysticks are moving OK but there's no control.'

'What about the other robotic workstation up in the *Destiny* module?' said Michael. 'We could go up there and try?'

Steve nodded, still trying to get the flailing monster arm under control. It yanked Ralph in one direction before flipping him over and pushing him in another.

Michael shot through to the *Destiny* module. 'This is

exactly the same as in the *Cupola*,' he muttered, switching on his screens and grabbing the controllers. 'Now, where are you Ralph…where has this mad robot taken you?' First, he spotted Marat, still edging along the rail towards the airlock they'd exited. Then after a few seconds of scanning the other screens, he noticed a white human-shaped figure, arms splayed like a skydiver, under the belly of the ISS.

'I'm here, Steve,' said Michael, impatient to get going. 'I'll take over and see if I can move Ralph.'

'OK. Go for it, Michael. It's been four minutes now and we really need to get him back in. Marat, keep making your way to the payload bay hatch and we'll try to get Ralph to you.'

Michael tried the first manoeuvre; just a simple up and down with the right controller and then left and right with the left controller. It worked. Then he tried the rotational and translational controllers. These allowed him to rotate an object and then turn it sideways. They worked perfectly. With the arm now cooperating, he soon got Ralph down to the right height, sideways and aligned with the payload bay.

Marat was waiting. He grabbed hold of Ralph's arms, pulled him forwards and clipped on a tether. Then he opened the payload bay hatch, still keeping hold of Ralph and, with the help of Michael's robotic arm, dragged him in. Marat then released Ralph's tether and closed the hatch door.

Michael raced down to the airlock where Steve and Buddy were waiting for the re-pressurisation to finish. As soon as the pump humming stopped Steve yanked open the hatch and they poured in.

'He's coming round,' panted Marat.

Ralph's groaning made him sound like an extra-terrestrial trying to communicate. Even when they'd removed his helmet he was drowsy and unable to speak.

'Hey, look at his hand,' said Buddy, pointing at a black burn mark on one of Ralph's gloves.

'Let's just wait until he's conscious first and then we'll take off his glove,' said Steve, pulling Ralph upright and gently patting him on the cheek. 'Come on, mate. Open your eyes. You've had us all worried like mad. Just give us one of your big smiles to let us know you're OK.'

Ralph took a few shallow breaths. His eyes flickered.

'What about you, Marat?' Michael asked, seeing exhaustion daubed across the large Russian man's face.

Marat stuck a thumb up; his head slumped against the side of the airlock.

Finally, Ralph's eyelids fluttered before lifting.

Steve sat him upright and pushed the water tube into his mouth. 'Just small sips, mate,' he said. 'Just take a couple of small sips and you'll be fine.'

Once he'd come round properly, Michael, Buddy and Steve helped Ralph out of the lower torso part of his spacesuit and called Sarah.

'God you really know how to scare someone,' she said, pretending to thump Ralph. 'What were you doing fooling around out there? You were supposed to be working.'

Ralph's broad, white smile returned for a few seconds until he saw Sarah prop herself against the side of the module wall and pick up her scissors. Steve slotted Ralph's feet under two floor straps before Sarah took hold of his scorched, right glove.

Designed to withstand the hostile environment of space, Sarah had to work hard to cut through enough material to slide the glove off.

'Ouch!' said Buddy, grimacing at the sight. 'That's some burn.'

'It hasn't breached the inner layer of the glove, so it's probably the heat from the explosion that's caused it, but it's still burned a nasty hole in his hand. We'd better get something on it straight away.' She pulled one of the medical kits from a drawer in the wall and unwrapped an antiseptic cloth.'

'Arghhhhhhhh! God that hurts!' shouted Ralph. He tried to pull his hand away but Steve held him firm until Sarah had finished.

'He should really go to a hospital with that,' said Sarah, screwing up her nose. 'He's only got saline and antiseptic cream on it – if he was at home, he'd have had it under running water for twenty minutes before it was even looked at.'

'That's a bit tricky up here,' said Steve. 'Do you think we're going to be able to treat it or do we need to get him down?'

They'd practised hundreds of 'what if' situations in training, but it hadn't crossed Michael's mind that this sort of thing really could happen. It would be bad enough if Ralph was out of action, but if they had to make an emergency descent, the whole mission would fail.

'How about asking me?' said Ralph, his left hand cradling his right like an injured animal.

'Sorry, mate,' said Steve, patting him on the back. 'We didn't mean to talk about you like you're not here. We're just worried. That's all.'

Ralph's usual swagger and confidence had gone and it was clear to Michael that he understood the seriousness of the situation. He rolled his eyes, shook his head and pushed out a large breath. 'Let's give Mission Control a call and get some advice from their on-call paramedic. If they tell us we've got everything on board to treat it, we stay, if not, three of us have to go home.'

'Good morning, John. This is Sarah Hutchins of the *Fortis*

crew aboard the ISS.' The screen in front of her flickered into life and Michael's mood brightened immediately. Next to John, sat Jamie; blond hair sticking up like wisps of beach grass. How could he look so relaxed when they were about to experiment with blood samples from his own mum?

'Good morning, *Fortis* crew. This is John Dell at NASA Mission Control. What can we help you with? We're not due to speak for another two hours. Is there a problem?'

Sarah recounted the incident with the robotic arm, the electrical blowout and Ralph's hand and put her question to the on-call paramedic.

The paramedic wanted to see the wound, before asking a whole load of questions from the colour of it, to the size of the blistering and whether Ralph had full sensation in his hand or not.

To Michael, it didn't sound good and Ralph's face agreed.

'Ralph, we need to give you painkillers and antibiotics, bandage you up and replace your dressing every three hours. If there's no change to the wound, you'll be fine. Any problems and we've got a different situation on our hands,' said Sarah.

Ralph nodded.

'Before you go, there are two things I need to mention,' said John Dell suddenly from behind them.

Michael had forgotten he was still there.

'You guys are going to have to give some serious thought as to whether the moon mission is still a feasible objective or not. Obviously, Ralph won't be able to command the mission now. Have a think about your options and let me know your decision later today so we can manage the logistics and media.'

Michael hadn't even considered this in all the chaos of the last hour. The very thing he came up here to do could be jeopardised all because of a freak accident.

'The other thing I need to tell you is just as important. Jamie verified that, shortly after Ralph's accident, both SSRMS robotic workstations were in use.'

'I don't understand?' said Buddy immediately. 'What d'you mean they were both in use at the same time? Isn't that impossible?'

'Thanks, John,' said Ralph, ignoring Buddy's question. 'We'll talk it through now and make our decision. We'll call back as originally planned and let you know. It'll also give us time to check the robotic workstations and see what happened this morning.' Then Ralph turned off the screen.

'Why did you finish the conversation with John like that?' asked Sarah, closing the medical box. 'Not more secrets?'

Ralph took his time answering. Either he didn't know what to say or he was trying to find a way of saying it, thought Michael, fiddling with one of the Velcro straps on the wall.

'Ok, let's take these one at a time,' said Ralph eventually. 'The first issue is whether we can still safely and successfully complete our *Vader* moon landing and sample collection.

Should he speak, thought Michael? Should he remind them that they'd spent eighteen months training for this mission; that the US was banking on this to re-establish itself as a world leader in space travel; that it was key for the European Space Agency to be involved in a mission of this stature and that this was what he had dreamed of for half his life? Even if all that wasn't worth it, surely they had to find a way to make it happen for Jamie's mum?

Buddy beat him to it. 'What if Steve takes over as mission commander? If he's confident he can do it, surely the mission is still on.

Ralph glanced at Steve, who nodded. 'We've got time

for you to take me through the mission plan. Marat knows what he's doing with *Vader* and Michael's all set for his sample collection. But we're still one short. We need someone to collect the extra samples with Michael.'

Michael couldn't imagine how devastated Ralph must be. He'd spent years training for this moment and a stupid accident had guaranteed that his name would be missing from the history books.

'Well that's got to be either Sarah or Buddy,' said Ralph quickly.

'Or we ask one of the Chinese crew,' said Marat. 'Ru or Shen could stay in *Vader* and I could help Michael.'

Even though they'd trained together for the past eighteen months, Michael still didn't know much about Marat. He said very little and always seemed so serious. It was almost impossible to know what to say to him and he'd never asked a single thing about Michael. Now Marat was suggesting that they take along a Chinese astronaut they'd only met the day before and who might be involved in the same research.

'Well it's an idea, Marat, but, given what we suspect, I don't think we can go there. It could be like handing them an advantage and taking a hit ourselves. I don't think there's any way we'd get that passed.'

Marat nodded but didn't reply.

'So we're back to either Sarah or Buddy,' said Michael, turning to both of them and shrugging. If he was honest he'd rather have an astronaut who'd been into space twice before than his fifteen-year-old best friend, but he kept the thought in his head.

'I'd love to get the chance to see the moon close up,' said Sarah, suddenly, 'but I have to get our samples ready today and start monitoring them before we do anything with the XO3. It'll have to be Buddy.'

Chapter Six

The only time Michael had seen Buddy this startled, was when Bob Sturton had told him he'd made it to the final three on the Children's Moon Program (CMP) eighteen months earlier.

'How about it, guys?' said Ralph. 'We wouldn't ask you if we didn't think you could do it.'

Steve and Marat nodded immediately. It took Michael and Buddy a few more seconds to get used to the idea before they did the same.

'That's it, then. Tomorrow morning the moon crew continue the mission as planned with Steve, Marat, Buddy and Michael,' said Ralph. 'OK, I'll confirm that with Mission Control later. We'll need to run Buddy through the mission scope but, in the meantime, let's get on with our schedules.'

'But what about the robotic arm malfunction? What d'you think went wrong? We'd better check it out, hadn't we?' said Buddy before Ralph had a chance to leave.

'I agree. I'm the next one out there to get the samples in and I don't really want to end up in that kind of state,' said Steve, pointing to Ralph's hand.

Ralph pulled at the threads on the end of his bandage.

'You know what happened, don't you?' said Sarah. 'You've got to tell us, Ralph – for everyone's sake.'

Ralph looked at the floor. 'All I know is that you can only operate one workstation at a time...unless the system is overridden in the central post. If that happens, then the robotic workstation in the *Destiny* module takes priority.'

'But if that's right,' said Michael, hardly daring to say the words out loud, 'it means...'

'Yes, it means that there was either a system blip that

we've never seen here before or...'

'...Someone switched control to the *Destiny* workstation and deliberately threw you around, Ralph,' said Steve, his eyebrows raised.

'Hang on a minute,' said Buddy, in a voice that sounded both indignant and panicked. 'The electric shock you got, Ralph...'

'The only switch to turn the power back on to that particular channel...' said Michael, suddenly on the same wavelength as Buddy.

'...Is in the *Harmony* node...right next to the *Destiny* module.'

Ralph nodded. 'That's where I'd got to.'

'Let me get this straight, mate,' said Steve. 'Are we saying that someone on the ISS deliberately set out to harm Ralph? If we are, there are only nine of us here and the *Fortis* crew were all with someone when it happened. That means we're looking at the Chinese crew.'

'I don't believe it,' said Sarah, red-faced. 'I don't believe that anyone would do that. We can't go making wild accusations and we certainly can't mention it to the Chinese team or anyone on the ground. We'll start a political war if this gets out. Can you imagine the headlines? "US accuse new ISS partners of science breakthrough sabotage." We'd be right in the middle of a nightmare.'

'So, Ralph and I will go and check both robotics systems and the power unit, if you're up to it?' said Steve, 'and then we can decide what to do next. Everyone else can just carry on as normal for now.'

'Are you nervous?' asked Michael, as they set up their exercise machines.

'Nervous...me?' replied Buddy, scrolling down the screen to find his programme on the resistance exercise device (RED).

'Yes, you.' Michael jabbed him in the ribs.

'How could *I* be worried about having to travel to, land, walk and then do some spade work…ON…THE…MOON! Ha…listen to me say that, dude…walk on the moon. How does it sound to you, Mike? Does it suit me?'

Michael couldn't stop the snort leaving his mouth.

'Feeling rough, Mike?' asked Buddy, strapping himself onto the machine and pressing the start button.

The words were stuck in Michael's throat and the tears… the tears weren't streaming down his face. They were doing something very different. His vision started to blur as a ball of tears began to form. At first, it was marble-sized and lodged in the corner of his eye but it soon morphed into a wobbly bubble of salty water. It grew so large that it eventually made a break for it across the bridge of his nose. Now he had one, single, hand-sized, clingy mass of water covering half his face.

'I've just got to get a picture of that,' said Buddy, his own tear bubble starting to grow. 'That is just awesome. I think the girls are going to love that look.'

It was a relief to laugh in the middle of all this serious stuff, thought Michael as they started their running and weightlifting programmes.

'Hey, Mike, what do you call a bicycle built by a chemist?'

'I don't know and don't really care,' said Michael as he started the first incline of his programme.

'Bike-carbonate of soda! Get it?'

'Crikey, your jokes are getting worse, Buddy. I thought Will's were bad enough. Where d'you get them?'

'Don't know,' said Buddy, curling his biceps as he lifted the bar to his shoulder. 'They sort of just come to me.'

An hour later, Buddy and Michael unstrapped

themselves from their machines and wiped them down with an antibacterial cloth.

'And here comes the first pitch of the day,' said Buddy, suddenly spinning his deodorant container end over end along the module.

'Will he be caught out on the first ball?' said Michael, bowing to his imaginary supporters and pushing himself back to catch the container. He barely touched it with the tips of his fingers. In earth's gravity, it would have dropped back into his hand and he would have made a victorious catch. In microgravity, just the touch of his fingers made the container jump up again like he'd given it an electric shock.

As Michael stretched to reach the escaping container, Buddy bounced around his imaginary baseball field and scored his first home run.

'Victory!' Buddy celebrated with a backwards somersault that ended up with him on his knees.

'Is this a private party or can anyone join in?' said Steve from behind them. 'You guys look like you're having fun. I think we need a bit more of that up here after what happened this morning.'

'Yeah, it was a bit heavy, wasn't it,' said Buddy, hitting the container towards Steve. 'Did you find out what happened in the robotics workstations and the *Harmony* node?'

'Unfortunately, it was just as we thought. The system had been overridden and there's evidence that the power for the outside electrical channel had been turned back on for a few seconds. Ralph and Marat have gone to see Ru and Shen.'

What would happen when Ralph showed them his hand? Would they have an answer for what had happened? Would they deny everything?

After three more rounds of the 'ISS deodorant roller baseball championships', it was time to find Sarah and begin their top-secret experiment.

'So what do we need to do with these samples?' Buddy asked, peering through the see-through plastic box they called the Microgravity Science Glovebox (MSG) and pointing to the rows of test tubes in a white rack.

'I'm just setting up. Then I'm going to fill the test tubes with PM4.'

Michael couldn't take his eyes off the small tubes in front of him. They'd soon be filled with something the world had spent decades trying to destroy; something responsible for millions of deaths a year and which was ruining Liz Matheson's life.

'Right, Buddy,' said Sarah, breaking Michael's daydream. 'I'm going to fill these twenty-four test tubes with PM4 and then I want you to add one pipette drop of the preservative in that bottle marked ROE to each.'

'What's ROE?' asked Buddy. 'I was all ready to be working on plant growth and the effects of radiation on cells. Sorry, Sarah, but this is all new to me.'

'No, I'm sorry. I'm in a world of my own. I'm still thinking about whether we should be doing this or not. OK, so we've got PM4 and we need to expose it to microgravity and monitor the changes. Some viruses and bacteria go ballistic in space. They grow much faster and become much more virulent.'

'Isn't that a bad thing?' asked Michael, concerned about the word 'virulent'.

'Not necessarily. Sometimes seeing how a virus reproduces and becomes stronger helps us work out how to make a vaccine or cure. So we look at what happens to it over the next couple of days and find out how it reacts.'

'So why the ROE?' asked Michael.

'OK. In the past, we've used a type of preservative called a "paraben". You find them in lots of things, like shampoos and makeup. They've got anti-bacterial and anti-fungal properties which can help us in space.'

Michael shrugged.

'You know I said that bacteria and viruses sometimes go mad in space,' said Sarah, pointing around the *Destiny* lab. 'Well, any bacteria or mould spores in the air here could damage our PM4 samples...'

'So we put a preservative in the test tubes to protect the sample,' finished Buddy.

'Exactly. We preserve the sample, allowing it to do whatever it's going to do in this microgravity environment. Rosemary oil extract (ROE) is just a natural replacement for the paraben we used to use. And all *you've* got to do, boys, is harvest enough XO3 for us to test on these samples. Either it doesn't work and no-one is the wiser...'

'Or it does work,' said Buddy, looking like he was about to start an exam paper, 'and we change the world.'

Sarah's steadied her right hand as she pushed the pipette through a rubber seal and squeezed a few drops of what looked like innocent water into the tubes. Once finished, she disposed of the pipette into a thick rubber bag attached to the side of the glass box and double-checked that the sample container was closed.

'Right,' she said, puffing out her cheeks. 'That's me done. Buddy, just give them a minute or two to settle, then you're on.'

With help from Michael, Buddy got into his TV detective-style protective suit, put his feet under one of the floor straps and pushed his hands into the tight, rubber gloves attached to the inside of the MSG. He reached to his left for the preservative. 'Is this stuff dangerous?'

Sarah smiled. 'When you're older and you start to lose

S. Y. Palmer

your hair, rub a bit of rosemary oil extract on your head. Apparently, it's great for stimulating hair follicles.'

'And the PM4?'

'Technically PM4 won't harm you unless it gets into your bloodstream, but we don't want to take any chances,' she said. 'If you're that worried, Buddy, I can take over?'

'No, I'm good,' said Buddy, swallowing. 'I've got this.' He pushed a fresh pipette through the seal, drew up some of the liquid and squeezed a drop into each of the test tubes. He steadily filled all twenty-four test tubes, replacing the lid on the container and doing the same as Sarah with his pipette.

'Well done, Buddy,' said Sarah. 'That was awesome for your first time.'

'Now what?' asked Michael.

'We wait,' said Sarah. 'I do my observations every few hours, look for changes and then we start the serious stuff when you bring back your XO3 samples.'

Michael gave a half-smile. Those few words suddenly made it all seem so real. To bring back the samples he and Buddy would have to go to the moon...and back. Could they do that? Could two fifteen-year-olds really go to the moon?

Chapter Seven

'What d'you reckon happened then, Mike?' said Buddy, on their way to the galley. 'A big bust-up with Ru and Shen?'

'I hope not.' Besides being a horrible situation, this was probably the worst place for a fight.

When they reached the galley, however, the atmosphere couldn't have been more relaxed. Sarah and Steve were pulling packets of food off the US and European racks and adding hot water from a tube on the wall.

'So now you're going to see why European cuisine is the best in the world,' said Steve, laughing. 'This is beef bourguignon with roasted vegetables.'

'And for the thing you call "dessert"?' said Ru.

'Sticky toffee pudding, like my mum makes,' said Steve, as if it was his own triumphant creation.

'Sounds most interesting and something we must try,' said Shen, nodding enthusiastically.

It was almost as if the events of the past few hours hadn't happened at all. Why were they all behaving as if they were the best of friends when the last time Michael had seen Ralph, he'd been off to accuse the Chinese of something terrible?

Steve must have seen the confused look on Michael's face, whispering, 'It wasn't them. They've got proof they were nowhere near the *Destiny* robotics workstation. It was just a malfunction and freak accident. There's no other explanation.'

'I think your European food has almost as much taste as Chinese food,' announced Shen. He laughed. 'It could have done with some ginger, soy and chilli but, apart from that, it was most agreeable.'

Michael loved the way that Ru and Shen found things 'most agreeable'. It was as if they'd learned English from old-fashioned books and dictionaries.

'Thank you,' said Steve, grinning, 'and I actually agree about the chilli.'

Ralph paused before changing the subject. 'So, we've heard amazing things about the construction of the *Dàdăn*. It took just three months?'

Shen nodded as he cleared away his rubbish.

'That's got to be some sort of record, hasn't it?'

'We needed to build quickly to fulfil our objectives,' replied Shen. 'Now we have been accepted as an equal partner on the ISS, there is so much we want to achieve.'

'Anything you can share with us?' asked Ralph.

Shen smiled. 'As you know, Ralph, China has plans to visit the moon and find solutions to the problems associated with human spaceflight. This is what we are concerning ourselves with.'

Michael kept his eyes down and sipped his hot chocolate. Shen hadn't given them anything useful. Why would he, anyway? The *Fortis* crew were sitting on a huge mission secret, so maybe the Chinese crew were too?

After he'd finished, Michael was straight on to the next thing on his schedule. He'd agreed to hold a video call with schools as part of his mission.

Although he was dreading being exposed live on screen, he was secretly excited to be sharing some of the fun things about living in space. He'd already worked out that he'd do the call from his sleep station and show the children around there first. Then Buddy would take the onboard video camera and they'd do a mini-tour of the ISS. It had been no surprise that most of the questions he'd received were about the toilet, food and how they slept at night. If only they knew what else was going on here.

'Er...hello...this is Michael May from the International Space Station, calling all children on the "May's Mission" programme,' said Michael, peering into his laptop screen and attempting a smile. 'I was lucky enough to be in the final three on the Children's Moon Program and get a place on this amazing mission. As you can see, I made it up here on *Inceptor 1* and I'm settling into my new home for the next eight weeks of the *Fortis* mission. Thanks for all the questions you've emailed me. They're really great and I'm going to try and answer some of them now. Then I'm going to give you a quick tour of the ISS.'

Michael turned away from the laptop and pulled himself from upright to upside down. 'As you can see, I'm just as comfortable this way round as the way you're sitting. My body doesn't recognise the difference. This is because I'm in microgravity, which is different from zero gravity. If you want to understand the difference and you're a bit of a space geek like me, you can read about it on my blog.'

Once he got over the initial lump in his throat it wasn't too bad. Staring at a screen wasn't half as scary as staring at real people.

'I've got a question here from Aida Evans in Lancashire. She's asking what it's like to sleep in space. Well, I've only had one night here so far but, I have to say, it's nothing like I imagined. For a start, you don't wake up with a dead arm or have to turn over because you're uncomfortable. There's no pressure on your limbs, so it feels like you can just totally relax your body and you're supported by the fluffiest, softest air pillow.'

He immediately regretted that last bit. He could imagine Jamie listening in at Mission Control or Charlotte in England or any of his friends having hysterics at his lame description.

'Er...let me show you around my sleep station,' he

said, trying to ward off the redness clawing its way up his cheeks. He unclipped his laptop from a hinged arm that was attached to one of the walls and panned around. 'This is my room. As you can see, it's not exactly a palace, but it's the only place on the ISS that I can call 'mine'. I've got some pictures on the wall, my own laptop and, for the duration of this mission, I'm responsible for looking after this.'

He held something red, white and blue up to the camera. It was Cyril, the mission mascot…a stuffed alligator. 'Cyril is watching over us and he's wearing his own special mission patch,' said Michael, turning the toy around to reveal the same symbol as the one on his t-shirt. For those of you who don't know, *Fortis* is Latin for brave. The alligator is the symbol of Florida, where our launch took place, and the colours represent the flags of each nation involved in this mission.

'So before I get my crewmember, Buddy, to take the camera and follow me around the ISS, I can take one question from the live audiences in Florida, London or Moscow. Sorry it's so late for those of you in Europe,' said Michael, glancing up at a chart. 'I'll be flying over you in about half an hour, so I'll say hello.'

'Hello. My name is Amy,' said a petite girl with tightly curled dark brown hair. 'I love you, Michael, and think you're awesome!'

This was his worst nightmare; someone he didn't know saying something mortifying live on air.

'Er…thanks, Amy…Er…did you actually have a question about the ISS?'

Amy didn't reply. She'd had her moment of fame on TV.

'Er…could I have a space-related question from someone in the UK, please?' Michael said, praying that this would be better.

'Hello there, Micky Moon. D'you remember me?' said a distant, yet horribly familiar, voice. 'I used to make your life at school a bit difficult sometimes, but I reckon it was me who toughened you up so you could do this space stuff.'

It was Darren Fletcher; the boy Michael had tried to avoid his whole school life in England; the boy who used to steal from his packed lunch and push him around. How had he managed to get himself on a live link-up to the ISS? Say something, you idiot, thought Michael, as he gave a forced smile and turned slightly away from the screen.

'Er…what a surprise,' he said, trying to stop flashbacks from crowding his brain. 'Er…I didn't think I'd hear from you, Darren. What d'you want to ask?' he said, dreading that it would be even worse than the 'I love you' girl.

'Yeah, I've changed a bit since you last saw me…you know…before you became famous and went to America to lead the celebrity life. I've sort of…I've sort of got interested in science and stuff,' said Darren, looking more uncomfortable than Michael had ever seen him.

The only sciences Michael could imagine Darren Fletcher being interested in were the sciences of bullying and torture.

'So what's your question then?' said Michael, deliberately abruptly.

'Yeah…well, it's about your onward trip to the moon,' he said.

Had he heard properly?

'Yeah…we know that travelling from the ISS to the moon hasn't been achievable until now because of the volume of fuel needed to get there. Can you explain the technology behind *Inceptor 1* which makes that possible?' said Darren, staring at the screen without laughing or making a stupid face.

Was this for real? It wasn't April Fool's Day, but Michael couldn't put the question with the boy who'd just asked it. 'Er…er…that's a really good question from the London audience,' said Michael, trying to compose himself. 'Basically, the question is how are we able to carry enough fuel to reach the moon from the ISS. OK, I'll try and keep this fairly simple. Just like the first stage separation after the launch of *Inceptor 1*, where we jettisoned the empty fuel tank and booster rockets, *Inceptor 1* has further stages which we're attaching up here. We've got the *Exploration Launch Stage*, the *Orbit Stage* and the *Exploration Return Stage* for each part of our journey. Each of these has a liquid core with smaller booster rockets, which will get us to the moon and back. Over the past few months supply vehicles have been bringing up those stages and they're now stored at two of our four docking ports. They carry enough fuel to get us into the moon's orbit and then to break us free and get back here.'

The look on Darren's face was something Michael had never ever seen before. He looked like he was genuinely interested.

'So you're building your own spacecraft up there?' said Darren, his eyebrows raised.

'Exactly. *Inceptor 1* is like a sophisticated piece of Lego. We're going to attach the stages, fuel modules and the lunar lander to it, ready for our moon mission.'

'Wicked!' said Darren, grinning at the audience. 'Thanks for that, Micky…um…I mean, Michael. I guess I didn't really take you seriously at school. It sounds amazing. Good luck. You sort of deserve it.'

Michael didn't reply. He was still in shock.

'Did you hear any of that, Buddy?' asked Michael, doing a fake knock on Buddy's sleep station curtain after he'd thanked his followers and logged out of the live video link.

Buddy pulled back the curtain in an upside down position. 'Did I hear it?' he said, giving one of his mischievous smiles. 'I watched it all. Priceless...I mean you don't have enough money to stop me sending that one around,' he said, laughing out loud at Michael's frozen face.

'You didn't?'

'Oh yes, I did! I logged on to see your video link, heard the gorgeous Amy proclaim her love for the super cool boy astronaut they call Micky Moon and caught the awesome way you dealt with bully boy,' said Buddy with a triumphant bow.

'You'd better be joking about sharing that around or you might find that Steve's recording of you chucking up your guts suddenly goes viral.'

Buddy smiled, slipping out of his sleep station and pointing the camera at Michael. 'So what do you want me to capture then?'

'I just want you to follow me and I'll do the rest. Just go where I go and please don't do any stupid voiceovers like you did in training,' said Michael.

'So moving out of our sleep stations, we're going to take you to Buddy Russell's favourite part of the ISS first,' said Michael, already moving. 'Buddy is behind this camera, in case you're wondering.'

In the galley, Michael explained the colour-coding system for food and how they either rehydrated or heated their food. He also held a few of the pouches up to the camera to show the different languages and whispered some of the crew's special treats.

After the galley, Michael glided through to the *Cupola* and Buddy pointed the camera downwards to capture what lay below the ISS.

'This is most astronauts' favourite part of the ISS,' said Michael, pointing to the swishes of cloud and coloured patterns below him. It's where you get an idea of how small the world really is and proof that it's round. It only takes us ninety minutes to fly around the whole world and this is our view.'

Buddy pointed the camera at Europe as the ISS passed over it.

'Amazing isn't it? You can't believe, to start with, that we're looking down on the whole of the human race but after a few hours up here, you recognise every continent you learned about in school and every ocean suddenly makes sense. You can join the whole lot up and really understand what the world is about.'

They were on their way to the airlock where Ralph and Marat had exited for their near-disastrous spacewalk, when Sarah suddenly appeared behind Buddy, waving her hands around like an over-excited parent at school sports day.

Michael waited until Buddy had paused the recording.

'What's up, Sarah?' said Michael.

'What's up?' she said, clutching her head. 'What's up is that something's happened to our samples. Someone's tampered with them and they're ruined!'

'What do you mean someone's tampered with the samples? How do you know that?' said Michael.

'Come on. It's easier if I show you,' she said, already heading back to the *Destiny* laboratory.

'Look!'

Michael peered down at the test tubes in the MSG and shrugged. As far as he could make out, these were the same test tubes that Sarah had filled with PM4 and to which Buddy had added the preservative.

But Buddy got it straight away. 'There should be four

rows of six,' he said. 'There's one missing.'

'Yes, but that's not all,' said Sarah, her eyes glistening. 'Look at the levels of fluid in them. They're too high, which means something else has been added. They're contaminated...ruined.'

'What else is in them?' asked Buddy.

'I've no idea. I can test for acid or alkaline and I can test for proteins but, apart from those, I'd be guessing. I can't believe it. Who would do something like this and why?'

Chapter Eight

'Do we have enough to start again?' asked Buddy. 'If we do, then we've only lost a few hours and you should still be able to log the results in time for the XO3 samples to come back with us.'

When did Buddy get so sensible, thought Michael? This was the boy whose humour had made the CMP bearable for him and here he was, giving his advice to an experienced NASA scientist.

Sarah examined the remaining PM4 sample container. 'I think we just about have enough to fill twenty test tubes, which is the minimum we'd need for a controlled experiment. Good idea, Buddy,' she said with a thin smile. 'Sorry I lost it. Yes, we can do the set up again, but I'm more worried about the missing sample. We've got to see Ralph and get to the bottom of this and quickly. We can't have PM4 loose on the ISS. It could be catastrophic.'

Michael stayed whilst Buddy and Sarah reset the experiment. She pulled the tray with the contaminated samples to one side. She still wanted to see what happened to them in microgravity over the next few days. Perhaps that would tell her what substance had been added. 'I know Ralph's resting,' she said, 'but I need to speak to him and I think you should both be there too. I don't want to do this, but I'm going to lock the MSG and take the key with me.'

Buddy and Michael nodded. It seemed the safest thing to do, even if it did feel awkward.

When Michael pulled back the sleep station curtain, Ralph's legs were in a foetal position, his hands out in front of him as if was sleep-walking.

'He looks like a cloth zombie,' said Buddy, pointing at

Ralph's hooded sleeping bag and bandaged hand.

The talking woke Ralph up with a start. 'What? What's...oh...it's you, Sarah. What's the matter? Has something happened?' He winced, pulled down his hood and unzipped his sleeping bag, stepping out into nothing.

Sarah told Ralph what had happened, or at least what she knew to be true, as Michael and Buddy waited in silence.

'Are you sure there were twenty-four test tubes?' was the first question Ralph asked.

'Positive.'

'You know what you're implying, Sarah, don't you?' Ralph said, with a 'here we go again' look on his face.

'Yes I do, Ralph. I know exactly what I'm implying. Someone on the ISS stole a sample, contaminated the rest and the only people who have anything to gain are the Chinese crew. There,' she said, her face flushed. 'I've just said what we're all thinking. Now, what are we going to do about it?'

'I don't know what you expect me to do, Sarah. It was bad enough asking Ru and Shen about the accident, but to ask them whether they've stolen our research and ruined our experiment...it could cause an international incident,' said Ralph. 'We're only just on good enough terms with China to allow them to become an ISS partner. Imagine what would happen if we suggested they were involved in theft and sabotage. Ru and Shen are two of the most respected men in the Chinese space industry. They're like celebrities at home. You've seen the posters.'

'But we can't leave it, can we?' said Sarah, bobbing up and down with frustration.

'No, we can't do that either.'

Michael cleared his throat as the most polite way of stopping Ralph and Sarah going round and round in circles.

'I don't know if it would work but Buddy and I could go and ask Ru and Shen for a look around their module. We could see if there's anything out of the ordinary.'

'Michael, that's a really good idea. Go and see Ru and Shen and find out what you can. Ask how their experiments are going and if you can have a look at any of them. Try and find out what they were doing in the last hour. I'll speak with Marat and Steve. Let's try and get this sorted tonight otherwise we'll have to think twice about any sort of lunar visit.'

Jamie's mum flashed into Michael's head. They couldn't abort their visit to the moon. It was too important. They had to find the missing test tube and fast.

'Ah, my *Fortis* friends,' said Ru from one of the computer stations on the wall. 'Do come in. You are always welcome in our *Dàdǎn* module.'

It was the first time Michael had heard Ru or Shen refer to the name of their module. *Dàdǎn* meant 'daring' in Chinese – the exact opposite of how he felt right now. 'Er… so how are things going in the *Dàdǎn*?' he said, hoping the colour of his face wouldn't let him down.

'Well, young Michael, we are so much enjoying our time on the ISS. We are learning much about the effects of microgravity on our bodies and we are planning more exciting research,' he said, quite naturally. 'How about you, Michael? What have you been occupied with?'

'Er…well, I've been doing some recording and answering questions from live audiences. It's been quite fun, actually,' he said truthfully. 'What I was wondering though, was if Buddy and I might be able to have a look at your lab experiments, please? I mean, this is also our first time in space and we're trying to learn as much as possible.'

'Oh, yes of course. It would be a pleasure,' said Ru. 'Let us give you both a tour of the *Dàdǎn*.'

The Chinese laboratory was immaculate. The metal surfaces gleamed. Nothing had been marked, stained, or scratched yet. Their MSG was also impressive. Twice the size of the *Destiny* version, it was a double box with a sliding glass partition so it could be used as two separate boxes or one very large one.

In one box Michael noticed vials of blood samples. In the other were rows of tiny green dots poking up from rectangular growbags.

'These are our plant trials,' said Ru. 'We're most proud of this. We've managed to accelerate plant growth by over two hundred per cent in a month by using a fertiliser impregnated with harmless bacteria. The bacteria grow far faster here and produce a much more effective nitrogen-rich fertiliser.'

'That's awesome,' said Buddy, looking at the specks of plant life in the box. 'That's got some serious benefits. Can you imagine growing every plant at twice the speed? At that rate, you'd give yourself a sustainable food source for a six-month mission.'

'Exactly, my friend.'

'And you'd be getting fresh food,' said Michael, already missing his favourite Florida fruits.

'Anything else?' asked Buddy, as if he'd suddenly remembered why they were here.

'We have one or two smaller tests to do on eyesight and the inner ear, but they will only take up a small amount of our time,' said Ru.

'I bet you've got really flash sleep stations,' said Michael, unable to think of a subtle way of asking to see them.

'Flash?' Ru frowned.

'Er...I mean smart.'

'You mean they are clever?' said Ru, looking even more confused.

'No, I don't mean smart...I mean...I bet they look new and modern and...shall we just go and take a look?' said Michael, already moving in their direction.

He was right. The Chinese sleep stations were amazing. First of all, there were six of them feeding off a central hexagonal node. Their wedge shape allowed astronauts to put their feet in first and sleep in an almost 'normal' earth position. On what they might call the roof they attached their laptops, pictures and any personal items. They also had a sophisticated light system that could simulate natural daylight.

'Twenty minutes before our alarms go off,' explained Shen, 'the unit starts emitting daylight. This brings us into light sleep so that we wake up easily and feel much better when the alarm eventually rings.'

'Awesome,' said Buddy, reaching into one of the sleep stations and craning his neck to look around. 'Wouldn't mind kicking back in one of these and listening to some tunes.'

'Yes, they are what you call "smart,"' said Ru.

'Why is that one closed?' asked Michael, pointing to the sleep station that went upwards from a central hole in the ceiling, like his.

'Ah, that is where Yue Shi is resting,' he said, putting his forefinger to his lips. 'She is suffering from space sickness too, Buddy.'

'She's still getting space sickness after a month up here? How's that even possible?'

'Yue has very kindly offered to take part in an experiment to do with the effects of microgravity on the inner ear. We decided that the person to do it would the one of us who suffered most when we arrived and that was Yue.'

'Well whatever you're doing to find a cure, it doesn't exactly seem to be working, does it?' said Michael.

'In fact, it is working perfectly well, my friend. We are trying to prolong Yue's sickness, so we can study it and make a fast-acting cure.'

'What? You're trying to make her sick?'

'No, we're not trying to make her sick, we're trying to understand what causes space sickness and in order to do that, she has to be suffering from it. We know that the human inner ear is very similar to that of the toadfish. They are very sensitive to even the slightest movements like we are, but they also have a remarkable ability to boost and reduce signals from the inner ear. If we can learn how they do it, then we can start to understand how we can do it artificially for astronauts.'

'So how do you prolong her space sickness,' asked Michael, sure that there was a flaw in this theory somewhere.

'Ah, that is the clever part,' said Ru, breaking out into one of his wide grins. 'Our balance is linked to the hair cell sensory organs in our ears. They help the brain to calculate when we are moving and also when we hear something. These organs have tiny little ear stones, which are made of calcium carbonate. They act as weights when there is gravity. When there is little or no gravity, they cannot do their job and our brains are confused.'

'Which is why we feel sick?'

'Yes, Michael. We can prolong the sickness by changing the amount of calcium carbonate in the ear because it fools our brains all over again.'

'But poor Yue,' said Buddy. 'If she's feeling half as bad as I did...'

'Yue's last day was yesterday. Now we let her brain do its natural job and stop her being sick.'

After finishing their tour of the *Dàdǎn* module, Buddy and Michael headed back to speak to Ralph.

'We couldn't find anything out of the ordinary and nothing that points a finger at the Chinese crew. Ru and Shen were doing experiments all day and Yue has been in her sleep station or the toilet most of the time.'

Ralph suddenly looked like someone had stolen the almost magical aura he usually possessed as commander of the ISS. Michael felt sorry for him but didn't have the words to help. Instead, he looked for that imaginary loose thread on his clothes to fiddle with.

Eventually, Ralph blew out several short breaths like he was trying to compose himself. 'We're...um...we're still on for the lunar mission tomorrow,' he said, nodding rapidly as if he was trying to convince himself. 'We've got a mission to complete, Jamie's mum to think of and we're going to do our best. You guys are key to this, so you'd better get your heads down for a few hours.'

Relief, worry, panic and doubt all fought for prime place in Michael's head as he set off to bed. He was supposed to be going on the first mission to the far side of the moon in the morning, yet as he pulled across his sleep station curtain, all he could think of was the suspicious accident and malicious sabotage that had marked his first twenty-four hours in space.

Chapter Nine

'Come on, sleepy head,' said Buddy's voice outside Michael's sleep station. 'It's time to greet the biggest day of your life.'

The last two years had seen so many 'biggest days of his life', thought Michael, savouring his comforting, safe sleeping bag. He'd been the only child in the UK to get onto the CMP, he'd made it to the final three in the world and, after eighteen months of astronaut training, he'd been selected, along with Buddy, to be the first child into space. If all that wasn't enough, he was also going to walk on the moon and return with a magical substance that might save Liz Matheson's life.

'Be right out,' replied Michael, putting on some music that Charlotte had sent him whilst he wriggled out of his comfy cocoon and reached for his laptop. If he was quick, he could video call his family before breakfast.

'Michael!' screamed Millie, when his face appeared in front of her. 'We miss you and love you and my friends can't wait to meet someone who's been to the moon. We've been looking at it, like, loads and I've bought these autograph books for you to sign. It's just going to be awesome!'

Typical Millie thought Michael. They'd only been in Florida for two years, but she already sounded American and was fully involved in every bit of US life. She was so busy with her friends, school, ponies and parties that she wouldn't think about asking him how he was. He missed her though – even her annoying habits of hogging the bathroom and singing too much.

'Hi, Mum, Dad, Granny. I thought I'd just let you know that I'm OK. I'm about to get ready for our far side mission.'

'How exciting for you, dear. Don't forget to wear a seatbelt and take some of those humbugs for the journey.

They'll help with your ears popping,' said Granny May.

If there were things that immediately reminded Michael of his granny, it would be humbugs, her pearl necklace, the funny smell of her bungalow in Presholm and the way she always squeezed him tight and called him 'dear'. He'd really missed her since they'd moved to Florida and couldn't wait to see her when he got back.

'I've got breakfast now and then we're checking over *Inceptor 1* and its new stages. Actually, if Millie's still there, I've got something to show her,' said Michael. He turned around and pushed his sleeping bag aside. Perhaps it was attached to his wall? Not there. 'Hang on a minute, it's probably under my clothes...don't look, Mum. It's even messier than my room...and as you can see, it sort of hovers and won't even settle in a nice pile.'

Michael moved around the few things in his sleep station. It only took him about thirty seconds to discover that Cyril was missing.

'Sorry, Millie, I was going to show you that I've got Cyril but Buddy must have him. I just wanted to let you know that I'm looking after him and that the crew appreciated your school's gift to us. He's kept us safe so far, so thanks. Tell your friends if you like.'

Millie let out one of her annoying-but-slightly-endearing shrieks, muttered something about telling Mary-Jo and ran off.

'That's sweet of you, Michael,' said his mum, smiling. 'She'll be dining out on that for days now.'

'We'll be watching, Michael,' said his dad from off camera. 'Take care and enjoy it – I'm sure you'll love it.'

'Will do.' As he clicked to end his video call he realised that the next time he called his parents he'd have been to the moon and back.

'Scrambled eggs or porridge?' asked Buddy, pulling packets from the food rack in the galley.

'Have we got any of those pancakes with maple syrup?'

'Pancakes...pancakes...yes, here we go. Pancakes with traditional Canadian maple syrup. Hot or cold?'

'Nicely warmed please, Mr Russell,' said Michael, helping himself to a pouch of juice while he was waiting.

'So how are you guys feeling?' said Ralph. 'Quite a big day for us all, isn't it?'

'Yup,' said Buddy, handing Michael his glistening pancake.

'Aren't you going to have anything?'

'Not sure I could keep anything down,' said Buddy.

'If you're feeling sick, you've got to let me use the toilet before you leave that evil stench in there again. Just smelling it makes me want to puke.'

'Thanks for the concern, dude. It's overwhelming. No, I don't actually feel sick now, but I reckon to eat scrambled eggs or porridge before a long, fast, bumpy ride, may not be the best thing to do.'

'Neither is arriving for a six-hour mining mission on the moon with nothing in your stomach. You've got to eat something, Buddy – preferably something that's going to keep you going for the rest of the day. Why not have some pancakes now and then something just before we leave?' said Michael.

'What are you – my mom or something?'

'I don't think so, somehow,' said Michael, poking Buddy in the ribs. He liked Buddy's mum. Carlie had always been really good to him. She'd helped him get to know the Florida area and had introduced him to friends of hers, who had sons the same age. She'd also put him up for nearly a month whilst his dad had gone back to England. He'd never forget those weeks of food, laughter and fun.

'Perhaps some pancakes would be OK,' Buddy said eventually. 'But it's you who's going to have to deal with them if they reappear.'

A different mood hovered in the galley this morning. Everyone understood what was at stake. What they were about to attempt had never been done before.

'So the first thing you have to do today is to check your kit, including seats and suits. Then we need to test our stages and *Vader's* systems. That's going to take a while. Sarah, I'd like you up in the *Destiny* robotics workstation whilst Steve and I go to the *Cupola*. Marat, can you please go to *Vader*, start the systems check and load the supplies and sample cases,' said Ralph. 'I just need a quick word with Buddy and Michael.'

What had they done now, thought Michael? Maybe Ralph had overheard Amy proclaim her love for him or seen them messing around in the galley?

'You told me that you don't believe that Ru, Shen or Yue have anything to do with the test tube sample of PM4 that went missing yesterday. Is that right?'

Michael looked at Buddy. 'I spent ages chatting to them last night and they didn't seem like they were hiding anything.'

Ralph nodded. 'Then without anything else to go on, we'll just have to be vigilant until we can find some answers. Right now we've got far more important things to concentrate on, like getting a small spacecraft with a brand new fuel configuration all the way to the moon.'

Marat had already equalised the pressure and opened *Vader's* hatch. He was sitting in the middle seat, cross-referencing his manual with the readouts on the screens in front of him. 'You are late. Come and sit down and go through these as I check them off,' he said, handing Buddy the manual. 'Leak checks are first.'

There was no warmth or friendliness with Marat – just work. Michael wondered what he must think of the rest of the crew when they told jokes or chatted about stuff at home. Did he think they were all clowns who didn't know how lucky they were to be here or did he just not get it at all?

'Sure,' said Buddy, sliding into *Vader* with one pull of his arm.

'And you can check the safety equipment and emergency evacuation systems, Michael.'

In many ways, this lunar lander, which had been twenty years in the design, wasn't much more advanced than the original *Eagle* from 1969. It still looked like a weird beetle-like creature with eight spindly legs. But these legs were groundbreaking inventions. The designers had taken nature, specifically the movement of crabs, as their inspiration. Instead of being static, *Vader's* legs could move in pairs, like the pincers of a crab, grabbing the moon's surface. It didn't matter if they landed on ice or on powdery soil. They'd still grip and hold *Vader* to the surface.

The rest of the exterior looked remarkably similar to the *Eagle*, except for the use of newer, more durable, impact and heat-resistant materials. It was inside that the time-lapse was most noticeable.

In front of Marat's chair was the command centre computer. This would allow him to monitor the usual things, such as speed, orbit and distance, as well as checking everything from the oxygen and carbon dioxide levels to the heart rate of the astronauts. Six 360 degree cameras were positioned around *Vader* and there was even a robotic arm and probe for any sample collections they needed to carry out from inside.

Michael checked the oxygen tanks, the carbon dioxide

removal systems and the emergency hatch mechanism. There was far less safety equipment on *Vader* than on *Inceptor 1* but the bit that worried Michael most was the lack of radio signal on the far side of the moon. If something went wrong, there'd be no way of letting anyone know.

Half an hour later they'd finished their systems checks and Marat repeated what Buddy would need to do once he climbed down *Vader*'s ladder and landed on the moon's surface.

Even though he'd heard this at least a hundred times before, hearing Marat actually say the words made the hairs on Michael's arms stand to attention.

'So I will get us to this area,' said Marat, pointing to their landing site on a map. 'It is very difficult terrain with many craters deeper and wider than anything you have ever seen. We will aim to land here,' he said, pointing to a gap between a cluster of circles, marking craters. This is the *South Pole-Aitken basin* and it is 1,600 miles in diameter. We will be landing just to the side of it, here. Once you are on the surface, I will lower the vehicle you have nicknamed the *Speeder* and you will reach the first site in less than five minutes.'

Michael loved the Star Wars nicknames that he and Buddy had given various parts of machinery and equipment. *Vader* came from *Darth Vader* and the mistaken belief that the part of the moon invisible from earth was called the dark side and *Speeder* was their name for the lunar buggy. These nicknames had stuck with most of the crew. What he and Buddy hadn't shared, however, was that Marat's hairy arms and chest made him a perfect *Chewbacca*, whilst Ru's small stature and formal way of speaking were similar to that of *Yoda*.

'Michael, I am going to ask Buddy to follow your lead when you get to the lunar surface. You will be in charge.

You know how much XO3 you need to collect and where you will find it. It is crucial that we get at least sixteen kilos and you must weigh each sample bag before you load it into the trailer. Is that clear?'

The boys nodded.

'Any questions?' said Marat, already closing his manual and shutting down the computer system.

'Only one,' said Buddy. 'How long do you think we're going to be up there?' he said, raking his fingers back through his gelled, black hair.

'It depends on how long it takes you to collect the XO3 and where Steve is in orbit. I think we will have about twenty to twenty-four hours there. Don't forget, we need to do some lunar mapping, testing and collect our water-rich samples too. After all, that is what we are supposed to be doing, isn't it?' said Marat.

'Actually, I've got a question as well,' said Michael. 'We're going to be on camera the whole time, so how do we convince people that we're only looking for water-rich samples and not a new substance that we believe will change the world?'

Marat smiled, which was a rare occurrence. But it was more a knowing and slightly smug smile than a kind one. 'Michael, when you watch back the recording, I don't think even *you* will be able to tell what you are collecting. All moon rock samples look similar. We expect them to be grey, powdery, with perhaps some subtle colouration, but no one will be able to tell what is inside the samples, so do not waste your energy on that. And please do not look worried on camera either.'

With *Vader* ready to go, Michael and Buddy carried out their own maintenance checks before going to help Sarah with the experiment samples.

'Everything OK here?' asked Buddy, peering around

S. Y. Palmer

Sarah to see what she was doing in the MSG.

'Yes, it's all good here. I've kept the MSG locked and I'm just testing the samples to see what's happened to the PM4 overnight.'

'And?'

'Small changes,' said Sarah, noting her results on a chart. 'Some really small changes to the protein structure as we expected. The protein should eventually sort of open up after a while here, a bit like a flower does and then we add the XO3.'

'And then the XO3 does its job?' said Buddy.

'Yes. Then the XO3 makes its way to the heart of the flower...and destroys it.'

Chapter Ten

'Two hours until launch,' announced Ralph over the *Destiny* speakers.

'Shall we go down to the *Cupola* and watch them finish testing the stage construction?' said Buddy to a subdued Michael.

'Er...could do...' said Michael but he wasn't sure he wanted to see the Meccano-type construction.

'Come on, Mike. Then we can get our seats and kit ready and get something to eat. We've got our Mission Control call in half an hour anyway, so we can't be long.'

'Have you got Cyril?' asked Michael, suddenly remembering his conversation with Millie. 'He wasn't in my sleep station and I thought we'd take him with us.'

'Sorry, dude. I can't help you there. I don't tend to need soft toys to go to sleep anymore.'

When they got to the *Cupola*, Ralph and Steve had almost finished.

'Looks like a totally different machine,' said Buddy, admiring *Inceptor 1*'s makeover.

'Yes, it's quite a beast again, isn't it,' said Steve, smiling at his handy work. 'Those rockets are going to give us a fair old shove.'

Each section had to be added in reverse. The *Exploration Return Stage* had been added first. That was the engine that would bring them back to the ISS. The *Orbit Stage* came next. It was far smaller; a thin band in the middle of the new spacecraft. It housed the booster rockets they'd need to get into and stay in the moon's orbit. Finally, the twenty-metre-long *Exploration Launch Stage* had been pushed into place.

'Booster rockets engaged,' said Steve.

'Running systems check,' said Ralph, watching the screen in front of him. 'Engagement confirmed. Systems are nominal.'

'Good afternoon, *Fortis* crew,' this is John Dell and Jamie Matheson at Mission Control. Do you copy?'

'Yes, Mission Control. This is Ralph Grant on the International Space Station. Good afternoon to you too.'

'Before we get to your briefing, how's that hand of yours doing?' said John.

There was no screen today, just the radio communication link, so John couldn't possibly see the bandaged hand that Ralph held up.

'It's about the same, John. It's still painful and a bit red but my onboard nurse assures me that it's heading in the right direction. Clearly, I'm disappointed not to be doing my tourist thing on the moon, but that's life.'

'Yes, we're sorry to hear that, Ralph. It looked like it was going to be perfect timing for you with this mission.'

'Thanks.'

'So we see your stage engagements have been successful and that systems are nominal. Unless anything occurs in the meantime, we're looking at a two o'clock pm GMT departure,' said John.

Michael looked at his watch. Just over an hour now.

'We'll be with you until you reach far side orbit and then we'll re-link as soon as the signal returns. Good luck, guys.'

No wonder John sounded so calm, thought Michael. He was sitting in front of a high-resolution TV screen that Michael would die for, nice and safe in NASA's hub. *He* wasn't about to climb into yet another new machine and travel a quarter of a million miles to a place without radio contact.

'Hello, Mike and Buddy. This is Jamie here. I want to wish you guys good luck. Enjoy it and make sure you get some awesome pictures to show me. Thanks for what you're doing.'

Michael knew what Jamie meant. Everything they did from now on had to work. They couldn't afford any mistakes.

'Hi, Jamie,' said Buddy. 'Shame the whole CMP crew couldn't be up here – it would be so cool. We'll do our best and hope your mom's OK.'

'And just a final few words from me,' said Bob Sturton's familiar drawl. 'Now y'all know what you need to do. Just go out there and do it as best you can. And remember to look around yourselves, guys, and hold those images in your head forever.'

With the call to Mission Control over, the boys changed into their flight suits and headed straight to the airlock that linked the ISS to *Inceptor 1*'s crew capsule.

'Are you good to go?' said Steve, rubbing his hands together.

'I think so,' said Michael.

'Sure am,' said Buddy.

'Of course, I am ready. I have been preparing for this whilst others have been joking around,' said Marat.

'So who do we have here?' said Ru's voice from the first hatch entrance. 'It looks like astronauts...and cosmonauts, ready for a big adventure.' He smiled.

Then Shen peered around the open hatch and into the airlock. 'Greetings, fellow explorers. The Chinese *Dàdǎn* crew would like to wish you a safe but exciting journey and we look forward to hearing your tales and seeing your amazing pictures.'

'Oh and we have good news,' said Ru. 'Yue Shi is feeling much better and is able to come and greet you.' Ru turned around and beckoned with his hand.

The much longer, black hair and slightly taller stature couldn't possibly disguise *her*...the person Michael loathed most in the world. She'd been at the centre of all the trouble on the Children's Moon Program. It was the cheat, the saboteur, the poisoner...it was Jia Li and she was standing right in front of him, two hundred and forty miles above the earth, pretending to be someone else.

'But...how...I thought,' stammered Buddy, as he flicked his head between the smiley-faced, long-haired girl in front of him and Michael's open mouth.

'What are *you*...?'

'Doing here?' she snapped, smiling immediately and making it sound as if Michael was stupid to even ask the question.

'I am part of the *Dàdǎn* mission. My name is Yue Shi. I am pleased to meet the *Fortis* crew. I have heard a lot about your exciting research projects,' she said, managing a smile without upturned ends.

Even the 'I'm pleased to meet the *Fortis* crew' sounded wrong. In fact, everything about this was wrong, thought Michael.

By the look on Buddy's face and his inability to form a single word, he was thinking the same.

'Pleased to meet you eventually, Yue,' said Steve, pushing himself over to her for an enthusiastic handshake. 'Glad to see you're feeling better. Sounded like you were in the wars.'

'In the wars?'

'Sorry – English expression. I mean you've been having a hard time over the last few weeks,' said Steve.

The imposter nodded. 'Yes, I have to say that it has been hard, but it is all in the name of science, isn't it.'

'Good afternoon, Yue. I am Marat Orlov. I am pleased

to meet you and I hope to talk to you when we return from our mission,' said the usually quiet Russian.

Was everyone going absolutely mad, thought Michael? They're saying hello to someone who isn't who she says she is and who had tried to get rid of her competition on the CMP. She was thrown off it…she'd tried to kill Aiko for goodness sake.

'Are you OK, Michael,' said Ralph. 'You've gone really pale like you've seen a ghost. Are you feeling sick?'

'Er…Er…no…I'm fine thanks. It's just that…'

How did he tell them that she was a fraud and cheat with a false name? With her history, *she* had to be the one who'd stolen the PM4 sample and ruined the others. It was obvious.

Another thought crept like moss across Michael's thoughts. What if the whole Chinese crew were in on it? What if they'd brought Jia Li or Yue Shi or whoever she really was to spy on them or steal their experiment results? What if Ralph's source was right and the Chinese were on the brink of a world discovery, which needed them to fail?

'Ralph, I need to speak to you before we leave,' he whispered, as Yue was introducing herself to Sarah and asking about the *Fortis* experiments.

'Sorry, Michael, we only have a small window to hit the right angle for our lunar orbit. It's going to have to wait until you get back unless it's a mission emergency?' said Ralph, nodding for Steve and Marat to board *Inceptor 1*.

'Well actually it is important,' said Michael, trying to order the words jumping around like pogo sticks in his brain.

'Mike, it'll wait,' said Buddy, bouncing over to him and pulling his elbow. 'Let's just concentrate on what we're doing here. We can sort other things out when we get back.'

Was Buddy right? If he left it and something horrendous

happened whilst they were gone, he'd never forgive himself, but if he spoke out now, they'd all be thinking about it when they should be concentrating on their mission.

Michael did his best to shoot a glare at Yue as he turned to board their lift to the moon. She returned something bordering on a smile. It was like a quick-fire game of chess and right now she was the ruthless queen who had all the best moves. He'd have to refine his strategy if he was going to beat her and he had just over two days in which to work it out.

Strapped back into something vaguely resembling the vehicle that had delivered them to the ISS, Sarah closed the hatch and Michael watched as the handle made its one hundred and eighty degree journey to *Locked*. Then the reduced crew of four signalled their readiness for Steve to begin the launch process. It would be different to their violent blast off from Florida. This time, instead of g-force, they'd experience the intense acceleration needed to get to the moon in just twelve hours.

'You did the right thing,' whispered Buddy, as Steve was reading out final checks for Marat to complete.

'Mm…' said Michael, partly annoyed at Buddy pulling him away from Ralph but also hugely relieved.

'Systems checked and nominal,' said Marat.

'Roger. Systems checked and nominal,' said Ralph over the radio. 'You're all good to go *Inceptor 1*. Keep in touch and have the second ride of your lives.'

'Ready for launch. Crew on standby,' said Steve, flicking the launch switches in sequence.

Michael pushed his helmet back into his seat, checked his harness and laid the palms of his gloves flat on his legs.

'And ten…nine…eight…'

He turned to the left to get one last look at the ISS. This mass of jumbled shapes and materials that looked so incongruous up here, the structure that seemed as if it might tumble down to earth at any point, had very quickly become almost comforting. He glimpsed his last view of the *Cupola*. Italian for 'dome', the *Cupola* was the most magical place from which to gaze down at his planet.

Something flickered at the window. It was a hand. Sarah was probably wishing them good luck with one of her energetic waves. But it wasn't Sarah. It was *her*. It was Jia Li or whatever she called herself these days.

'Seven...six...five...four...'

She was waving with something in her hands. Michael couldn't make it out until he noticed the colours: red, white and blue. She had Cyril, the mission mascot. She must have stolen it from his sleep station. And there was that sinister smile again.

'Three...two...one...and we have lift off.'

The acceleration pinned Michael to his seat. They'd have at least an hour of this before they'd reduce the thrust. It was the only way of reaching the moon's orbit in time.

'Crew status?' said Steve.

But before anyone could answer John Dell's voice invaded Michael's headset.

'*Inceptor 1*, this is John Dell from Mission Control. This is not a progress report. I repeat this is not a progress report. Please copy.'

'Copy, Mission Control. This is Steve Winters. Go ahead.'

'*Inceptor 1*, this is an emergency call to alert you of a metre-wide meteoroid, closing on you at thirty thousand miles an hour. We've mapped an asteroid collision on one of our high-resolution telescopes and it's produced a meteoroid, which is heading straight for you. You must change course immediately to the coordinates we've just sent you.'

Michael shot a glance out of the window, half expecting to see a boulder hurtling towards him.

'*Inceptor 1*, please confirm that you have changed course in accordance with our instructions. You have approximately six minutes until impact.'

Chapter Eleven

Steve said nothing, but they only had six minutes to get out of the way of this piece of rock that was fizzing towards them. Why was he hesitating?

'Mission Control, I'm looking at the screen and I think the situation's changed,' said Steve, assuming manual control and tapping in new coordinates. He immediately increased the thrust and angle of inclination, throwing the crew backwards.

'This is Mission Control. We've detected multiple meteoroids. You've got a full-blown meteoroid storm heading your way. We've worked out a path through and are sending you three sets of coordinates. Steve, you're going to have to follow these precisely to avoid a collision. We're going to be helping you through this from the ground.'

Michael tried to picture what would happen if just an edge of one of the meteoroids caught *Inceptor 1* on its way past.

Buddy closed his eyes, alternating between holding his breath and taking a rapid gulp of air.

From the way Mission Control had described it, any minute now there would be a rapid burst of rock bullets coming their way.

'First meteoroid twenty seconds from impact. Increasing inclination to seventy-eight degrees and reducing thrust,' said Steve. 'Hold on everyone.'

The manoeuvre was the equivalent of slamming on a car's breaks and yanking the wheel to one side. Michael shot forwards and then to the left. He'd hated the hours of lying still to make the plaster cast mouldings for his seat but, right this second, it was the only thing keeping him from being flung around the inside of the spacecraft.

'Wish I'd not eaten so much now,' said Buddy, his gloved hands clamped tightly around his seat edges.

'No, Buddy. You are not, under any circumstances, going to throw up. There is far too much going on. Just hold it.'

The spacecraft juddered like a building in an earthquake and Michael was slammed against the side of his seat again. For a split second the window was filled with something… and then it was gone.

'Was that what I think it was?' said Buddy, staring out into the black.

'Second object thirty seconds from impact. Increasing thrust and reducing the inclination to forty-three degrees,' said Steve.

Inceptor 1 responded immediately, lifting Michael upright again then throwing him back in his seat. As the meteoroid shot past them, *Inceptor1* shuddered in what felt like the after draft of a colossal lorry.

'Two down and one to go,' said Buddy, his face now resembling the colour of a church candle.

Michael nodded but there was still one piece of rock careering towards them.

'One minute to impact.'

'Mike?' said Buddy.

'What?'

'If we make it through this and get back safely, I'm going to try and find my dad. Promise me that if I get cold feet, you'll remind me what I said up here?'

'I promise and…for what it's worth, I think it's the right thing to do. I'm sure your mum will understand if you tell her it's what you want.'

'Thirty seconds to impact. We're staying on full thrust but increasing inclination to ninety degrees…now.'

'If we get back,' said Michael, 'I'm going to tell Ralph everything I know about Jia Li and try to find that missing sample. There can't be many places to hide it. I'm not going to let her get away with it and I don't want you to stop me, Buddy.'

'Agreed. Just be careful, Mike. You know what she's capable of.'

At thirty seconds there was no shudder. They waited. Nothing.

'Meteoroid averted,' announced Steve.

Was that it? Were they safe?

'Mission Control, this is Steve Winters of *Inceptor 1*. Please confirm that the meteoroid storm has passed and that the flight field is now clear.'

'Roger that, *Inceptor 1*,' said John Dell. 'The meteoroid storm has passed and your flight field is clear. Well done, Steve. You were amazing up there. You're good to continue your journey.'

Michael heard cheers, whoops and laughter in the background for just a few seconds before the link disappeared, but celebrating was the last thing on his mind.

Buddy's face agreed.

'Well done for keeping your cool, crew,' said Steve. 'Now let's see if we can have a really uneventful rest of the flight, shall we?'

The trajectory was reset, the thrust increased to eighty per cent of the original level and they continued their journey.

Michael let his eyelids roll down and cover his eyes but his brain fluttered like a butterfly behind them.

Sleep must eventually have smothered Michael's worries as he woke to hear Steve's announcement that they were decelerating ready for insertion into the moon's orbit. He peered out of the window nearest to him, straining to get the first view of his favourite celestial body but, even though there were millions of bits of plasma out there that people called stars, it still remained a big, dark nothingness.

'Starting retro burn,' announced Marat.

This manoeuvre reversed the engines, slowing them enough to allow the moon's gravity to pull *Inceptor 1* into its own orbit.

Steve jettisoned the stage one booster rockets.

Michael was expecting the bang this time and caught sight of the long propellant tubes falling away to one side.

'Ready for insertion into lunar orbit,' said Marat.

The minute he saw it for real, every black and white picture, poster and video he'd ever seen as a child became irrelevant.

This was so much more than Michael had expected; more beautiful; more graceful...perfect.

'There's your moon, Mike,' said Buddy, knowing what this meant to his friend. 'Pretty awesome, isn't it?'

Michael didn't speak. He couldn't. Most people talked about the moon being a grey, pockmarked, dusty ball, but they were wrong. The patchwork of colours in front of him ranged from white, through light grey to dark grey and almost black. Up close there was no 'man on the moon' face, but craters that were thousands of miles wide and mountains that would make it into the top ten highest on earth.

Without the intermittent firing of the engine, it was also silent – a perfect way to see the moon for the first time.

'Insertion into lunar orbit complete,' said Marat, as if he was declaring a finished crossword.

Michael wondered what it would take for Marat to get excited about something. If it wasn't this, what was it?

'So, we'll just do our leak checks and then we can get out of these seats and have a stretch,' said Steve.

Maybe a stretch was exaggerating, thought Michael. Even though there were only four of them, the crew capsule was rammed with equipment that wouldn't fit into the service module. Extra food packs, oxygen canisters and water containers had been wedged into every gap around them.

'Oh...this is good,' said Buddy, lifting up his arms until they touched the roof. 'I feel like someone's screwed me up like a paper ball and then sat on me.'

Michael nodded. They were like a cluster of chrysalises hatching. He pulled himself over to the porthole window and waited until the hypnotic sight came back into view.

'Once we've had a chance to move around a bit, you'll need to use the facilities and have something substantial to eat before we programme our lunar descent,' said Steve.

'What he means is go to the bathroom, stuff your face and get ready to walk on the moon,' said Buddy.

Steve joined Michael at the window. 'Special, isn't it? I had an image of what it might look like, but this is something else. It's like a different world. Seems a shame to walk all over it, take what we want, deposit our rubbish and then leave.'

'I know what you mean. I'm not sure how I feel now I'm actually here,' said Michael. 'I mean, it's a total dream come true and everything, but I wonder if something like this should stay a dream. That way nothing and no one can spoil it.'

'I had this poster on my wall – Neil Armstrong and Buzz Aldrin on the moon. I used to tell my parents that it would be me one day,' said Steve, smiling. 'But as time went on and life went by, I knew that very few people were interested in the moon any more. There were far more exciting places for humans to get to, like Mars or Venus. The moon sort of became unfashionable and people pretty much stopped talking about it.'

'But you were a fighter pilot, so you must have known you might get a chance to become an astronaut?'

'Yeah, I suppose I knew that my job wouldn't harm my chances if the opportunity came around, but the British aren't that well-known for space travel and I assumed I'd be at the end of a long list if there was ever another mission to the moon. When I applied six years ago, I never really thought I'd get to this point. Anyway, the fact is that both of us deserve to be here, but we've got a much more difficult job ahead of us than we thought. Good luck, Michael. I think you're amazing and you're one of the few other people on this planet – well, I mean on that planet,' he said pointing to the roof of the *Inceptor 1*, 'who feels the same as I do about visiting the moon.'

The final preparations for lunar descent took place in silence. Even Buddy was unusually quiet.

'Right, we've checked our orbit coordinates,' said Steve, 'and we're on target to reach the descent spot in thirty minutes. I suggest you board *Vader* now. Once you've confirmed that your systems are nominal, Marat, we're ready.'

'Marat nodded, opened the second hatch leading from *Inceptor 1* and disappeared.

Everything they'd run through on the ISS was then repeated. Marat was meticulous about following the manual and Michael sensed Buddy's boredom. They checked the EMUs that Buddy and Michael would be using for their spacewalk. They counted the sample bags, which would be equally distributed around *Vader* to maintain its stability when they left the moon and they ran through their supplies of oxygen, food and water.

'There can't be much on this thing we haven't checked or tested,' whispered Buddy.

'If you need to say anything on board,' said Marat, 'please say it so we can all hear it. If it's not mission-critical, there is no need.'

Michael thought about saying, 'Yes, Sir' and Buddy saluted like they were in some sort of lunar army.

Steve poked his head around the hatch door. 'All set?'

'Systems and equipment checked,' confirmed Marat.

'Then I'll close the hatch. Good luck guys...and Michael...enjoy it,' said Steve.

Once in their seats, Steve's voice came over their headsets. *'Vader*, this is *Inceptor 1*. We are nine minutes from lunar descent. Do you copy?'

'Roger,' said Marat. 'Nine minutes and counting.'

Their orbit coordinates had to be perfect before they could commence their descent; otherwise, they could end up anywhere in the fourteen million square miles of the moon. An inaccurate descent would be like landing in India, instead of China.

The timer display reached zero. 'Commencing descent,' said Marat.

'Roger,' replied Steve. 'Take it nice and easy, Marat. I'll be tracking you for a few minutes before we lose radio contact. Good luck.'

This was it. They were on the final part of their journey to the moon.

Michael could see *Inceptor 1* directly above them on the screen and their landing site, a circle with *Fortis* written in it, below.

Descent involved a combination of gently letting themselves drop towards the moon without going too fast or losing control. Marat could activate the booster rockets to provide some upward thrust if they were coming down too quickly, but Michael knew he'd want to preserve their fuel for the return to *Inceptor 1.*

'Twenty metres until impact,' said Marat.

Why did he say that? Impact was normally a negative word and this was going to be the most amazing experience ever. Why didn't Marat say 'twenty metres until we see the most wonderful natural satellite creation in the entire universe'?

'Ten metres…five metres…'

The booster rockets slowed them down slightly, like a gentle press on a car's breaks, before Michael felt a jolt.

'*Inceptor 1* and Mission Control, lunar descent is complete,' said Marat.

With no radio signal from the far side of the moon, Mission Control wouldn't be able to hear this message live. Michael pictured the banks of nervous families waiting to hear that they'd landed. Not only that, a sudden thought darted across his mind. Apart from their temporary short-range contact with Marat, Michael and Buddy would soon be completely alone on the surface of the moon.

Chapter Twelve

The view from *Vader* was more stunning than any sci-fi movie set Michael had ever seen. The powdery, grey, dusty soil stretched out in front of them for a few hundred metres, before it dropped away into the *South Pole-Aitken basin*. Beyond that, vast mountains towered in shapes not found on the weather-beaten earth.

'Take a look at that!' said Buddy, following Michael's gaze. 'Awesome isn't even enough. Look at the mountains and the soil and...oh my god, Mike...we're on the moon. We're on the actual moon!' Buddy's face said it all.

'I knew it would live up to what's in here,' Michael said, tapping his head. 'No, it's even better.'

'Engines are locked off. Leak checks complete. You can now take off your helmets and prepare for your walk,' said Marat.

'Don't you think it's amazing,' said Michael suddenly. 'Don't you think it's the most wonderful place?' he said, not getting Marat's almost casual approach to having landed on *the moon*.

'I think maybe we have more beautiful places in Russia,' he said, 'but we are not here to marvel at the landscape. We are here to do a job for which we have been trained, so let us make the most of the time we have here and ensure we do it properly.'

Getting ready for a spacewalk in such a confined area was a challenge. Michael and Buddy soon worked out that they could only do it one at a time.

'Communications check,' said Marat, his voice suddenly booming into Michael's headset.

'Check,' answered Michael.

'Check,' said Buddy.

'Have you made sure you can reach your water tube?' said Buddy, his already twisted towards his mouth.

Michael nodded.

Marat pulled at parts of their suits to check that they were properly sealed. Then he tested the oxygen and carbon dioxide removal systems and finally the computer readout on the front of their suits.

'Are we nearly good to go?' asked Buddy.

'You will be ready to go when I say you are ready,' replied Marat. 'This procedure has to be done properly. You are going to be out of contact for most of the spacewalk, so you must be as well prepared as possible. Were you asleep during this part of your training perhaps?'

Michael flicked Buddy a 'better be quiet' look and the rest of their preparation took place in silence.

Some of the larger equipment had already been loaded on to the lunar buggy they'd named *Speeder*, but the smaller tools had to be clipped to tethers and loops on their waists.

'We look like futuristic DIY cowboys,' said Buddy, slapping a hand on each tool at his side, like they were guns.

'Here are your maps,' said Marat, clipping two identical, plastic cards to Michael and Buddy's waists. 'The samples appear to be concentrated in relatively small areas and once you get down there it will be easy to get disorientated.'

Marat didn't need to tell Michael any of this. He'd studied the map before leaving the ISS and on the journey here. He was familiar with the layout of the area around them and the distance between the circles of highlighted ground. These were the areas that had a similar geological blueprint to the place where XO3 had first been found.

It was time to go.

Marat sealed the hatch to the command module and the boys were suddenly alone, with only a thin layer of metal between them and the moon.

'Good luck, Mike,' said Buddy, offering him a gloved high five.

'You too.'

Buddy turned a large, metal wheel, which released the lander descent bay door and nodded to Michael.

Michael placed his glove on the door and pushed until it reached ninety degrees. The moon's surface stretched out in front of him like a vast wonderland. Not even Disney could think up something as spectacular as this.

Getting out of the lander was more difficult than it looked. He had to exit in reverse, lowering his foot until it met the first rung of the ladder. Then he wrapped his gloves around the handles on the outside of the lander and brought his other foot out. There were only six steps left – only six steps until he was standing on the moon.

He paused and glanced up at Buddy, who smiled and gave him a thumbs-up.

Climbing down the last two steps without falling backwards took every bit of concentration. He turned around slowly and looked at the alien world in front of him. 'Lunar descent complete,' he panted, repeating the words that Mission Control had told him to use. 'The Fortis mission is proud to announce that NASA has returned to the moon. This is Michael May from Great Britain,' he said, feeling his throat tighten. 'I am honoured to be part of the NASA mission and to represent children from all over the world who have aspirations of getting into space. I encourage you all to follow your dreams – you never know where they'll take you.'

Buddy was next, following Michael's lead down the ladder. 'This is Buddy Russell from the USA. I'm lucky to have been given this opportunity at the last minute. I aim to do my best up here for you all and to make my country proud.'

'Marat, this is Michael. We're ready for the *Speeder* to be lowered. Do you copy me?'

'Roger that,' said Marat. 'Lowering sequence commenced.'

There was no 'well done' or 'how is it out there, guys?' or any words of encouragement from Marat. It was like working with a robot.

Michael and Buddy watched as *Vader* deposited the *Speeder* like it was laying an odd-shaped egg. *Speeder* was another of their nicknames but, instead of flying above the ground like in the Star Wars films, their version had four oversized rubber tyres and a trailer for their mining equipment.

Buddy used an extendable metal pole with a capture hook on the end to pull the *Speeder* out from under *Vader*. He was already panting. If this was hard, how difficult would it be trying to dig out sixteen kilos of XO3 and ten kilos of water-rich samples, thought Michael?

Once they'd checked the *Speeder* over and connected up the solar panels, it was time to go.

Michael raised his leg in an attempt to get it over the *Speeder* seat, but he couldn't lift it high enough and lurched forwards. Buddy stifled a laugh as Michael tried again. 'It's no use, Buddy; you're going to have to help me get my leg up and over the seat.'

'No problem,' said Buddy, kangaroo bouncing over to Michael.

It must have looked comical to anyone watching but they had no idea how hard it was to do anything in these suits, thought Michael, trying to bend at the knee.

'Right, you're on now,' said Buddy. 'The only problem is that I need to get on behind you.'

Somehow, after trying different methods and after lots

of leaning forwards, leg-lifting and bouncing, Buddy was on too.

Michael fired up the *Speeder* and craned his neck to look behind.

Buddy nodded.

'Proceeding to site one.' Michael pulled back the throttle and moved off past *Vader*.

Buddy squeezed him around the waist and Michael knew what that meant. Neither of them could quite believe that, at fifteen years old, they were riding a motorbike-buggy across the moon.

From their simulator sessions at NASA, they knew the ride would be bumpy, but nothing had prepared them for just how deep some of the craters were. They made the potholes in English roads seem like tiny dimples, thought Michael. Even with rubber wheels that looked like giant doughnuts they were shaken, jolted and banged each time they went into and then out of a crater. The *Speeder* didn't react like it would on earth either and each bounce was exaggerated, making them go up higher and then come down with a bigger bang. It must have looked like a slow-motion action movie.

'On the left,' said Buddy, after five minutes of bone-shaking.

'Got it.' Michael spotted a cluster of small mounds in an S shape. 'I'm going to stop in the middle of the mounds and we can work one way first and then the other.'

With no proper weather on the moon, the mounds were grey swirls of pockmarked rock arranged in intricate geometric shapes. The closest to this on earth would probably be the ice drifts in the Arctic, thought Michael as he came to a halt.

Getting off the *Speeder* was almost as tricky as getting on it. Buddy was able to slide back to where the trailer joined it, but Michael needed help again.

They checked their maps to make sure they were in the right location, drawing a line between the two curves of the S shape. Along this line was where they'd find the first deposits of XO3 – if the imaging from the recent flyby had been accurate.

'This is Marat Orlov from *Explorer 4*,' came the voice over their headsets. *Explorer 4* was the official name for *Vader*. They had to use it whenever their conversations were due to be broadcast. 'It looks like you have found the first site and seam of water-rich soil. You'll have about an hour there before you need to go to site two. We are going to lose contact just before you reach it.'

Michael paused. If only the world knew that the few samples of water-rich soil that they'd bring back from the moon would be dwarfed by the kilos of XO3 they were looking to harvest. 'Roger that, Marat,' he replied, already lifting up the hinged lid of the trailer to get out their equipment and sample bags. The 'normal' soil would be collected and sealed in airtight boxes to preserve the samples but the XO3 would go into thick, heavy-duty bags, made of similar material to their spacesuits. It was vital that any contamination was kept to a minimum and that they avoided coming into direct contact with the XO3. Despite Sarah telling them that it shouldn't be harmful to healthy cells if it could wipe out cancer cells, what other damage could it do?

If their information was correct, they were likely to find the largest deposits of XO3 in an area that had a pinkish hue.

Buddy scanned the knobbly, grey soil. 'Can you see anything, Mike?'

'Not yet. Let's move over there and have a look.'

The boys shuffled and bounced, searching for the tell-tale signs.

It was Buddy who saw it first. On the flat, just before one of the mounds, he pointed out a patch of soil that was definitely a different colour to the surrounding area. 'Do you think that's it?' he said, scuffing the soil with his foot.

'It could be. Let's remove the top layer and have a look.' Michael wrapped his hands around the spade. The pressure inside his suit made it awkward to hold and his hands had to work hard to keep their grip. 'Shall I start digging first and you hold the bags?'

'Sure and when you've had enough just say and we'll swap over.'

At least they wouldn't have the same problem as Ralph and Marat. Although the gravity on the moon was less than on the earth, there was still enough of it to prevent their equipment from floating off.

Michael had seen the footage of Buzz Aldrin and Neil Armstrong collecting moon rock samples on the first landing in 1969. He'd noticed how they'd struggled to bend and thought that a fifteen-year-old might be better at it. How wrong he was. Bending at the waist was difficult in an EMU and bending at the knee, almost impossible. In order to get down to the ground, it was a case of pulling back his knee as far as it would go and then leaning forwards until he could push the spade into the soil.

Buddy was clearly finding it just as difficult, trying to position the bag as close to the spade as possible and having to jump around like a life-sized puppet to get in the right position.

Michael scraped back the soil on top and pushed the spade down as far as he could. The ground was so hard that he started to doubt whether they'd be able to get anything in the sample bags, let alone sixteen kilos.

The pink colour came from a shiny, almost crystal-like substance. It looked a little like the quartz crystals his sister collected. She'd love it. If it wasn't so deadly, he could imagine her wanting to make jewellery out of it or having pieces displayed on her bedroom shelves.

'So that's what we're here for then?' said Buddy, leaning forward to look at the substance that NASA hoped might change life on earth. 'If you can get any big pieces, I'll just pick them up. It'll save having to lug around a load of soil as well.'

Finding large samples, however, proved to be difficult. They broke quite easily and the boys ended up putting large amounts of soil in the bags with the crystals.

'How are we gonna know whether we've got sixteen kilos if we're putting in soil as well?' asked Buddy.

'The sixteen kilos assumes that we're just digging in sample-rich soil and putting the whole lot in the bags. If we can sift out some of the crystals on their own, we'll end up with more than we need,' said Michael, his arms already screaming from the exertion. 'Let's wait until we've got as much as we can here, then we'll weigh the bags.'

An hour of digging left the boys hardly able to talk. They'd got themselves into a system, which seemed to work and talking was an unnecessary activity.

'This is Marat Orlov from *Explorer 4*. Are you on schedule to move to site two?'

The voice made Michael jump. He was in his own world, concentrating on doing the job and trying to preserve his energy. He hadn't even had time to really take in the new world he'd just landed on. 'Er…yes, Marat. We're just about finished here. Give us five minutes and we'll be moving to site two.'

'Oxygen and CO2 levels are good. Any problems?' asked Marat, with his usual lack of concern.

'No, we're all good here, Marat. How are you?' replied

Buddy.

There was no answer. That was it. They were on their own. No radio, no contact, nothing. Were they now the loneliest duo in the entire universe?

Chapter Thirteen

Locating the second site was easier. It was in the centre of a semicircle of mounds and Buddy spotted the pink tinge immediately. 'My turn to dig, Mike.'

From the first spadefuls, Michael pulled out several hand-sized pieces of XO3 and the sample bag was soon bulging.

'I reckon we've got more than one bag full there,' said Buddy, puffing as he spoke. 'Maybe we can make do with fewer bags?'

Michael felt like Buddy sounded. They both took regular sips of water now, only talking when they had to.

It'd only been two hours since they'd left *Vader* but Michael felt like he'd done a major work out in the gym. Everything ached and his hands felt like someone was rubbing a wire brush across them.

'I'm with you,' said Buddy, when Michael suggested a quick break. They couldn't sit down in their spacesuits but they managed to lean against the *Speeder* and stay still for a few minutes.

Michael surveyed the Asia-sized landscape. The moon had never appeared like this in his head because he'd always imagined it from the earth. From there, it was small, smooth and almost round, with white, grey and black swirls. Up here it was a different place. For a start, the ground, hills and craters all contrasted brilliantly with the darkness of space. It didn't look real at all and he could see why some people had been suspicious of those first images of the moon landing. Also, the ground was far more uneven and cratered on this side than he'd ever imagined. Right this second he knew the moon less than ever before; a stranger rather than the friend he'd expected.

'Are you good to go again, Mike?' said Buddy, trying to stretch in his spacesuit, but looking like he was doing some sort of weird dad-dance.

Michael blew out a long, slow breath and blinked several times to try and clear his eyes. He'd struggled to sleep the night before and was paying for it now.

'Yeah. Let's get another few shovels of soil here and then head off to the final site. That's where the flyby saw the largest density of water-rich samples.'

As they bounced and were shaken like sauce bottles, the final site came into view. It had a different landscape altogether. It was situated at the base of a rock cliff, shaped like the crest of a mammoth wave. The rock curled over them as if it had been frozen instantaneously by dry ice.

'That is so totally awesome,' said Buddy, bending as far as his suit would allow to look at the underside.

'Not if it falls on you, though,' said Michael, pulling the equipment out of the trailer for the last time.

'It's probably been like that for millions of years. Look, there are no bits of debris on the floor and it's pretty much intact. Guess that's what happens when you don't have weather coming through.'

'We're trying to find these patches of ground,' said Michael, showing Buddy their map. 'It looks like they're right at the base of the cliff, where there's no light and the temperature is about minus two hundred and fifty degrees. If there's ice, there must be water.'

Buddy nodded and the two of them continued in silence.

It was Michael's turn to dig and for the frozen soil, they needed an ice pick as well as a spade. He could hardly operate his limbs any more. It felt as though someone had twisted and pulled them and then made him do squat thrusts and press-ups for hours.

Despite the exertion, the boys collected the water-rich

samples relatively quickly, breaking off chunks of frozen ground and sealing them in containers. But finding the last three bags of XO3 was too much.

'I've got to have another rest,' said Buddy, trying to crouch but performing an awkward bow instead.

'You can't. We've got to be back at *Vader* in under an hour and we're two kilos short. Come on, Buddy, just a bit longer and we can have a good rest.'

The final two kilos sapped whatever tiny amount of energy the boys had left.

'You go and start up the *Speeder* and I'll throw this lot in the trailer,' said Michael, seeing the pale face inside Buddy's helmet.

There was no bounce left in Buddy and his walk to their transport was more of a shuffle accompanied by the forwards occasional lurch. He rested both hands on the handlebars and pressed the switch to bring the *Speeder* to life.

Nothing happened.

He tried again.

Nothing.

'Press down with your left hand and then flick the switch on your right straight up,' said Michael.

'What d'you think I did?' snapped Buddy. 'It didn't work...hang on...I'll try it again.' Buddy repeated the startup sequence, but the engine remained lifeless; not even a little splutter to suggest it was about to fire up. It was dead – like a used battery. 'Now what d'you suggest?' asked Buddy, as if he expected Michael to come up with the answer. 'What are we supposed to do miles away from a lunar lander we can't contact?'

'It's got to be something simple,' said Michael, running through the operation briefing they'd had on the *Speeder*. We need to check to make sure the air intake isn't clogged with dust. Wasn't that the number one reason for it to break down?' Michael inspected the intake grill. 'It's completely covered,' he said, removing it, banging out the grey enemy and replacing it. 'Try again.'

Nothing.

'Oh my god, Mike,' said Buddy. 'What are we going to do? We're stuck here with this piece of space junk and all this useless garbage in bags, with no way of getting back. If we can't work it out, we're going to run out of oxygen before we get to *Vader*; even if we could walk that far.'

The same panic seeped into Michael's head. Buddy was right. If they couldn't get the *Speeder* to work, that would be it. They'd be famous for being the first children on the moon...and the first to die on the moon. He had to think of a way out.

They'd completed a survival simulation as part of their training but that had been in Alaska, where there were animals and trees and abundant water. Here, they had rock samples that might contain tiny amounts of water. Even if they could extract it, how could they use it – take off their helmets and drink it? The other item they'd collected wasn't even worth thinking about. It might be a super-substance on earth but it was worse than useless here.

'We've got to head back,' said Buddy, unable to stand in one spot and breathing noticeably harder.

Michael didn't reply. He couldn't let Buddy's panic affect his decision. If they started to walk back Marat would soon realise there was a problem and come and get them. But did *Vader* have enough propellant to get here and then back up to rendezvous with *Inceptor 1*? He had no idea. If it didn't, what would Marat do? He thought about it again and he *did* know what Marat would do. He'd save himself and leave them.

'What if one of us stays here and one of us tries to make

it back to *Vader*,' suggested Michael?

'I'll go,' said Buddy, already turning away from Michael.

'Well let's just think about that for a minute, shall we,' said Michael, trying to work out how to say no to Buddy. He checked their oxygen levels. 'I don't understand,' he said, blinking rapidly and shaking his head to clear it. The gauge on Buddy's tank showed a far lower reading than his and Buddy's carbon dioxide levels were far too high. That's why he was struggling to breathe and acting strangely.

'I want to go, Mike,' said Buddy. 'I need to go back. I'm not feeling great and I don't think I can...'

'It's OK, Buddy,' said Michael, attempting to put his stiff, unresponsive arm around Buddy's shoulders. 'We'll go back together. We'll stay together...no matter what happens.'

Buddy said nothing, standing with his head bent forward, like a marionette without its operator.

Michael searched through the equipment on and around the *Speeder* and its trailer for anything of use. He attached the pickaxe and spade to his belt loops, more as something positive to do in front of Buddy, than something he actually thought would help them. Nothing else was of any use. It was daylight for another week, so there was no need for a torch and the rest of the stuff they had was connected to the stupid samples they'd been collecting.

All of a sudden this surreal, dreamland of a place looked barren and stark. There was no one and nothing here to help them and, for the first time, Michael saw the object of his dreams morphing into the stuff of nightmares.

'Come on, Buddy. Let's get back to *Vader*,' said Michael, in the same voice he used with Millie when she was watching something scary on TV.

'How long d'you think it'll take us?' asked Buddy,

already stooping and shuffling rather than walking.

'Er...it probably won't be that long before Marat realises something's up and comes to find us,' said Michael, desperate to believe his own words.

They hopped, stumbled and jumped in silence, following the *Speeder's* tracks. They had to keep their heads low because the sun was like a fiery theatre spotlight in their faces. Even with reflective visors, it dazzled their weary eyes.

It took Michael another three or four steps before the thought reached his brain. That was it. 'The sun!' shouted Michael at a totally bemused Buddy, who'd dropped down into a semi-press-up shape.

'Help me up, Mike,' he slurred. 'What's the matter with you? I thought we were helping each other back to Marat?'

'We are...I mean we were...I mean we're not, we're going back!' shouted Michael in a rush.

'What? What d'you mean, Mike? We need to go forwards, not backwards,' said Buddy, steadying himself enough to set off on his own.

Michael took four kangaroo bounces to reach Buddy and yanked him to a halt.

'What are you doing, Mike? Let me go. I've got to get back!'

'Buddy, just stop for a minute, please. I want to talk to you. I've got something important to say and then we'll carry on, OK?'

Buddy looked at Michael with desperate eyes.

'Buddy, listen to me,' said Michael, pulling Buddy's helmet to make him concentrate. 'I think I know why the *Speeder* didn't start.'

Buddy stared.

'It's the solar panels.' Why hadn't he thought of this when they'd first had a problem? He could have saved them all this panic.

Buddy still didn't get it.

'We put the *Speeder* by the rock face whilst we took our samples and loaded up the trailer. It was in the shade the whole time with the ignition on.'

Buddy nodded and Michael assumed he finally understood. But Buddy started walking again.

'Buddy! It's solar-powered. It needs sunlight to work and we left it in the shade. All we've got to do is pull it out into the sun for a bit, get the solar panels to recharge and we can get it to start.'

For a few seconds, Buddy kept shuffling forwards. Then he stopped.

'Come on, Buddy. Let's get back and get the *Speeder* into the sun. Give it five minutes and we should be OK to start heading back.'

Michael felt the tightness in his throat and stomach relax slightly at the thought of getting the *Speeder* to start. He just hoped it would work. If it didn't, he had no idea how Buddy would react.

Getting back to the spot they'd left was quicker. There was at least some hope in this direction.

'It's stuck,' said Buddy, lifting his arms in the air. 'It's no good, we can't do it.'

'Hang on a minute.' Michael leaned forward and pulled out handfuls of grey powder and bits of rock from under the front wheels. 'Check all around it, Buddy. We've got to remove anything obstructing the wheels before we try to get it out.'

It was like collecting the samples all over again and the flood of lactic acid built quickly in Michael's arms. 'Let's take the trailer off too and make it as light as we can.'

Soon, they were ready to try and move the *Speeder*.

'You push, Buddy and I'll pull,' said Michael.

Buddy did as he was told and got ready at the back.

'One...two...three...push!' said Michael, holding onto the handlebars and pulling them towards him, knowing his life depended on it. 'And again.'

This time the *Speeder*'s wheels seemed to rock forwards and slightly out of the groove they were in...but then fell backwards again.

'It's not going to work, Mike.'

'Try again, Buddy. Come on. If we can do this, we'll be fine. Come on. Help me.'

They tried twice more before Michael could see that Buddy was on the verge of giving up.

What could he do to get Buddy to try again?

'Think about what you said to me, Buddy. Think about what you said. You told me that if we got back safely, you'd contact your dad. That's what you said, Buddy. So, let's have one more go, get this thing moving and get back to Marat. Then you'll be halfway to getting back safely and speaking to your dad. You want that, don't you, Buddy?'

Buddy stared at Michael with glassy eyes, put his hands on the back of the *Speeder* and nodded.

Michael counted again and pulled as hard as every sinew, muscle and tendon in his body would allow.

The *Speeder* rose up out of the indent it had been sitting in...and stayed there.

'It's coming, Buddy. Push again. We're on the flat now so it should be easier.'

The pushing and pulling inched the *Speeder* forwards until it was almost rolling.

'Keep going, Buddy. We're doing it.'

In silence, the boys kept going. All Michael could think about was getting back to *Vader*. Nothing else mattered right now. He'd collect whatever they asked him to if it meant making it back.

Chapter Fourteen

Michael soon felt a change in temperature on his helmet. They could only be seconds away from total sun. 'That's it. We've done it,' he said, still leaning on the handlebars for support.

Buddy wobbled around on the spot like a skittle that had received a glancing blow but hadn't decided whether to fall down or not.

It was like waiting for exam results, thought Michael. You were desperate to find out, but half dreading the answer. 'Let's give it a couple more minutes.' A couple more minutes sounded nothing really, but they were probably the most important of their lives.

Buddy didn't want to try the engine, so Michael put his hands on each side of the handlebars, held down the start-up button and flicked up the switch with his right hand.

The *Speeder* hummed its whiny start-up tune but did nothing more.

Michael tried again. This time there was definitely a little more of the humming, but it didn't progress to the full-blown engine sound. He'd give it one more go. That's all he could manage.

The hum began…and then the engine coughed into life.

Buddy steadied himself before going back to drag the trailer onto the *Speeder*.

With heavy panting and loud groans, they managed to help each other on. Michael moved the throttle forwards and they were off. He blinked furiously to stop the water in his eyes from obscuring his view. As he stared at the *Speeder's* tracks in front of him, the exhaustion that was folding over his head like a sorcerer's hood was kept at bay by his determination to get them back safely.

Buddy had his arms wrapped around Michael's waist; his helmet slumped on his shoulder. He didn't move or say anything, even as Michael pushed the lever up to maximum speed and bounced them violently in and out of deep craters.

They sped past the *S* shape mounds where they'd stopped for their first sample collection and were soon approaching the *Vader* landing site.

'Hold on, Buddy. We're nearly there.'

But as Michael guided the *Speeder* around the final corner, expecting to see the crab-claw legs anchoring *Vader* to the moon's surface, there was nothing. It must be the tears, he thought. They'd blurred his vision. He shook his head and blinked, but the view was the same. *Vader* wasn't there.

He was sure this was the right place. He pulled up and checked the map in case he'd missed something...but he hadn't. This was their landing spot. He could even see the long pulls of the crab claws. *Vader* had been right here.

Buddy was either asleep or had passed out from exhaustion. Either way, Michael could do nothing. He had no intention of waking him to explain that they were right back where they started hours ago – with no hope of getting back to the ISS.

'Marat, this is Michael. Do you copy?' he said, trying not to allow his voice to rise along with his panic. Nothing. He tried again, but there was no answer from the Russian.

'Are...we back yet?' asked Buddy from behind him in a voice that was slow and slurred.

'Nearly, Buddy,' lied Michael, scanning each direction for their mini spaceship. There was nothing to see, but Michael was sure he could hear something. It was like the short bursts of heat from an air balloon on an otherwise totally still and quiet morning. It wasn't until a shadow darted across his helmet, making him flinch, that he realised *Vader* was coming down right above him.

'What?' he shouted, revving the engine and surging forwards to avoid being squashed.

Vader's six dainty jets of fire slowed its descent until it landed.

'Look, Buddy,' said Michael as the crab claws closed their pincers and *Vader* fell silent. 'We're here. We did it.'

Buddy raised his head from Michael's shoulder, stared at *Vader* for a few seconds and then slumped back.

'Marat, this is Michael. Do you copy?'

'This is Marat. Where have you been?' came the unfriendly voice.

Michael's eyes were hot again. He couldn't find the right words to answer Marat's question. 'There's something wrong with Buddy's oxygen and CO_2 levels. I'm going to get him into the descent bay now, attach the *Speeder* and then jump in myself. You're going to have to help me, Marat.'

'Let me know when you have sealed the hatch and I will start the pressurisation of the airlock,' said Marat.

Getting Buddy into *Vader* took Michael far longer than he wanted. It was like moving an awkward-shaped sack. With the oxygen and CO_2 canisters on Buddy's back, Michael couldn't grip him properly. The only thing that helped was the reduced gravity – without that, it would have been impossible.

Michael propped Buddy against the side of the ladder whilst he pulled himself up. His arms burned, his legs screamed and his head felt like someone was turning a screwdriver around inside it. How different these six steps felt now.

Once the hatch was open Michael had to come back down the steps, reattach the *Speeder* to *Vader* and then push

Buddy up the ladder with his shoulders. They collapsed like huge white dolls with clumsy, stiff limbs that didn't work as they should.

'Come on, Buddy,' panted Michael. 'Marat's going to sort out the pressurisation in here and then we can get you some proper air.'

There was no response from Buddy. His eyes were closed.

'Pressurisation complete,' said Marat.

Before he did anything for himself, Michael took off his gloves and broke the seal on Buddy's EMU. As he twisted off Buddy's helmet he released a waft of pungent, foul-smelling heat.

'Come on, Buddy. You've got to help me. I don't think I can get you out of this on my own,' said Michael, taking off his helmet and stretching his neck from side to side.

Buddy didn't speak but gave a flutter of a smile, lifting his arms in the air for Michael to release the lower torso of his EMU.

Eventually, both boys were back in their flight suits, their dusty space suit parts scattered around them like a teenager's bedroom floor. Michael pulled the pile over to one side so they could open the hatch to *Vader* and noticed the spare suit on the floor. It was almost as dirty as theirs now – covered by the clouds of moon dust they'd just brought in with them.

As soon as Buddy was through the hatch, Marat had the oxygen ready for him. 'Just take long, deep breaths. We need to get you stable again,' he said, snapping the elastic holding the mouthpiece over the back of Buddy's head. 'I will check his tanks.'

'Where were you, Marat?' Michael asked, still confused about events. 'You weren't here when we got back.'

'You were not here when you should have been. You

were over one and a half hours later than the agreed time. I had to try to find you. Without a radio, there was no way of knowing if you had had an accident.' He looked away and busied himself with the readout from Buddy's oxygen and CO_2 canisters.

'But you were coming from the other direction?' said Michael.

'I had to look everywhere. So I went off in one direction, before coming back and then going in the opposite direction,' said Marat. 'The main point is that you are both safe. Buddy looks better now. It seems that there was a fault with his breathing apparatus. His oxygen tank wasn't at premium levels and his CO_2 removal system was only operating at fifty per cent effectiveness.'

'What does that mean?' asked Michael.

'It means that he was being slowly starved of oxygen and poisoned by CO_2,' said Marat.

'Will he recover?'

'Yes, he will be back to normal in an hour or so, but he wouldn't have wanted to be out there any longer.'

Michael looked at Buddy, who was slumped in his seat, his eyes still closed.

'You've been through it, haven't you? But I told you I'd look after you, didn't I? Just take it easy now. We've done the hard bit and we'll be off to rendezvous with Steve soon.' He looked out the window and questions pushed into his weary head. What did the moon mean to him now? Would he look up at it when he got home with his old feelings of awe and wonder, or would his thoughts now be tinged by the loneliness and panic he'd just experienced? Would he ever feel the same about the moon again?

It was going to be nearly seven hours before *Vader* could rendezvous with *Inceptor 1*. Although he didn't want to be cooped up with Marat in a tiny vessel on the moon's surface, Michael was glad to have a bit of time for Buddy to recover. He could also prepare for the communication with Mission Control that would happen almost as soon as they got back with Steve. They'd have to give an interview to the camera showing their excitement about the mission. Right now, that was the last thing he felt like doing. He also wanted some time to stare at his fantasy satellite outside; to look at the terrain and to picture where he was on his favourite poster of the moon at home.

Buddy was buckled into his seat, asleep. He'd woken temporarily, guzzled a litre of water, wolfed down a sugary snack and gone straight back to sleep again – probably the best thing for him. Michael craved sleep too, but his head was crammed full of questions, like why had Marat gone in the opposite direction to find them? Why not follow the map?

Michael inspected his red, puffy hands with patches that were missing skin. He'd worn these gloves in training before, but never for this long or for such physical work.

'We must take our photographs now,' said Marat, dragging Michael out of his thoughts. 'We have good light and we can get right over the *South Pole-Aitken basin* if we are lucky. We just about have enough propellant.'

Michael would be in charge of the camera, which he'd really been looking forward to. Like a mini version of the robotic arm on the ISS, the end boasted a high definition 360-degree camera. He'd practised using it by standing in the doorway of his room at the Florida Space Center and getting the arm to move forwards and round the corner into Buddy's room. He'd taken pictures of Buddy reading his latest sci-fi book – right up until he was treated to a rude facial expression.

Buddy was stirring. Colour had started to reappear in

his cheeks and Michael knew he was feeling better when the first thing he did was to check the state of his gelled, black hair. It was his 'trademark' and it had to be 'just so'.

'Man that was hairy,' said Buddy, looking around *Vader* as if he hadn't seen it for an age. 'What happened to me, dude? It feels like I've just gone ten rounds with a heavyweight boxer and then slept for a week.'

Michael smiled and his shoulders fell a little. 'You nearly gave me a heart attack, Buddy,' he said, holding out a biscuit.

'Sorry, Mike. I don't really know what happened. One minute I felt absolutely fine and the next I could hardly breathe. Something wasn't right.'

'Yeah, Marat said there was some sort of malfunction with your oxygen and CO2 levels.'

'But everything was working perfectly when we checked them before launch and, anyway, Marat checked the EMUs again here, didn't he?'

'Are you ready, Michael?' said Marat, marking the end of the boys' conversation. 'Once you are harnessed in I will take us over the basin. You need images of the approach and then we want pictures to show the scale of the crater.'

Michael switched on the robotic arm and grabbed the controllers.

'Arghh!' He let go. It was as if someone had held a branding iron on his fingers.

'D'you want me to have a go?' asked Buddy, shrugging. 'I'm not saying I'll be as good as you but I could try.'

'No, it's OK, thanks. I just need to get these things moving again,' said Michael, still wincing at the screaming in his hands.

To test the camera, he swivelled the joint at the end of the arm so that it was facing *Vader* and took a series of images. When they appeared on his screen, the reality hit him. They were a quarter of a million miles away from home, on the far side of the moon in little more than a flimsy, metal container.

'Ascent rockets engaged,' said Marat. 'Lifting off the lunar surface and proceeding to *South Pole-Aitken basin*.'

Michael couldn't wait to see it. The far side was littered with vast holes but this one, at 1,600 miles in diameter, was one of the most extensive impact craters in the solar system.

Delicate rocket bursts eased them off the moon's surface and the rear-facing rockets then pushed them forwards. Soon the camera picked up what looked like a dark mass below them; except this wasn't a mass…it was a hole. Several miles deep, it dwarfed anything the earth could offer. No one had ever seen anything quite like this, let alone look into it.

'Let's hope we don't run out of propellant,' said Buddy, grinning. 'Imagine falling down into that. It'd be like disappearing into the mouth of some freakish space creature.'

Michael eventually got his hands to cooperate. He took masses of images of the crater rim and along the bobbly, rough edges that vanished into nothing.

'We will spend another five minutes over the crater,' said Marat. 'Take as many images as you can.'

'There's no point,' said Michael. 'We've lost sight of the crater edge now and the camera can't focus on black. I'll wait until we come back over the rim and try to get some shots then. Those are going to be the most interesting and give us more accurate measurements.'

'If you're short of good images,' said Buddy, smiling and framing his face with his hands, 'there's always me.'

Michael smiled. He knew Buddy must be OK again if he was joking around.

On the way back to their take-off site Michael captured the sweeping edge of the crater. It was like someone had crimped two edges of pastry together, like a Cornish pasty. Whatever had slammed into the moon must have been epic-sized to create a hole like that, thought Michael.

He took a few last images of their landing site and what they could see from it, before using their in-flight camera to take some of the crew. Every photograph would be around the entire world within seconds of them being back in radio contact, so he tried to capture *Vader* and its three passengers as best he could.

'Do you want to smile, Marat,' said Michael, pointing the camera at him.

Marat had his head in the flight manual, going through the sequence for their moon orbit rendezvous.

'Marat?'

'Just take the photograph, Michael,' he said, not even looking up. 'I have no interest in being in front of the camera. In case you have already forgotten, you and Buddy nearly perished out there. This is not a game.'

Michael took some shots and returned to Buddy. 'Why is he so vicious? He doesn't need to be like that.'

'I think it's just his way.'

'But I don't know how he thinks this is a game for me,' said Michael. 'It's anything other than that. Just because we're not his age, he thinks that we're playing at it. It wasn't him out there that could have died.'

Chapter Fifteen

'Twenty minutes to rendezvous with *Inceptor 1*,' said Marat. All of a sudden his mechanical-sounding words felt almost comforting. Even though they were only transferring from one spacecraft to another, Michael couldn't wait to see Steve and return to the ISS.

On one hand, he was sad to leave the silvery sphere he'd been gazing at from his bedroom window for years. He could have easily spent another few days exploring its mystical far side. On the other hand, he now understood that the moon was a force of nature. Maybe it didn't exist for humans to explore or conquer. It had shown them its cold, unforgiving nature – perhaps a clever ploy to deter people from returning.

Before they could leave the lunar surface for good, Marat had to detach the descent gear. This included the engines and landing equipment that had got them down from *Inceptor 1*. More rubbish left on the moon, thought Michael, straining to see out of his window as Marat decoupled the descent stage from *Vader*. They were now an even more insignificant dot in the universe, with tiny booster engines to lift them off the surface of the moon and back into lunar orbit.

As they rose quietly Michael caught sight of that famous view from the moon; the mottled blue, green and brown sphere they called 'planet earth'. The image he'd had as his screen saver for years appeared right in front of him right now.

His silent wonder was interrupted first by a crackling on the radio and then by an instantly recognisable voice.

'*Explorer 4*, this is *Inceptor 1*. Do you copy?'

'Copy *Inceptor 1*,' replied Marat. 'This is *Explorer 4*. We are in lunar orbit and ready for rendezvous. Ten thousand metres and closing.'

'Roger, Marat. It's good to hear your voices. I hope you had an amazing trip and got what you needed. I'm going to guide you into contact and capture. Let's just take this nice and easy,' said Steve.

Michael had never been so glad to hear someone's voice. It meant that they weren't alone. More importantly, it meant they had a way of getting back to the ISS.

'*Explorer 4* docking probe aligned. Reduce thrust to 5 metres per second...1 metre per second.'

There was the slightest of bumps as the two spacecraft became one and the familiar process of docking, equalising pressures and checking the seals began. Steve opened the hatch on his side first before Marat did the same from *Vader's* side. It wasn't as momentous as their arrival at the ISS but, in a way, it was more of an achievement. They'd avoided a catastrophic meteoroid storm and just escaped the prospect of being stranded on the moon.

'You first, dude,' said Buddy. 'I owe you.'

Michael didn't wait to be asked again. He unclipped his harness and pulled himself towards the hatch as quickly as the room around him would allow.

There was no need to transfer the XO3 and water-rich samples to *Inceptor 1*. New technology allowed them to take *Vader* back to earth to be reused. Michael had no idea when the next mission to the moon would be. It probably depended on whether these samples contained a magic ingredient or not.

'So how was it?' said Steve, his face hopeful and eyes wide. 'How did it feel to land on the moon, Michael? I bet it was the most brilliant sight ever. And what about actually walking on it and touching it?'

Michael smiled a small, thoughtful smile. 'It was

amazing,' he almost whispered…truly amazing.'

'Yeah, well apart from…'

Marat didn't allow Buddy to say another word. He slapped his finger to his mouth and glared at him. 'We collected our geological samples as planned and took some useful images of the *Aitken basin*,' he said in a mechanical way as if he was explaining a maths question.

Why was he behaving like this? And why was he keeping what had happened from Steve? Michael got his answer as soon as the red radio transmission button lit up. They'd moved around in their orbit and had suddenly come back into radio contact. Everything they were saying could be heard by Mission Control and any second now, their moon landing would be broadcast to billions of people around the world.

'This is John Dell at Mission Control. Do you copy *Inceptor 1*?'

'This is Steve Winters on board *Inceptor 1*. Yes, we hear you, Mission Control. We can confirm a successful descent to the lunar surface, approximately two hundred metres from the *South Pole-Aitken basin*.'

The instantaneous whooping and cheering forced Steve to stop and the four astronauts waited.

What were they supposed to do or say? Michael didn't feel like cheering and the noise was jarring. It was like someone celebrating a cup final they hadn't even been to.

'Michael May and Buddy Russell completed a successful moonwalk and sample collection,' finished Steve.

Michael imagined Jamie standing up and pumping the air, delighted for his friends and hopeful for his mum. Bob Sturton would be nodding and smiling to know that his training and hard work had paid off.

'Congratulations to the crew of *Explorer 4*. Perfect landing and great rendezvous with *Inceptor 1*. Please stand by for footage of the lunar landing. Transmission to networks will be in approximately thirty seconds,' announced John Dell.

It would only be thirty seconds before his family, friends and strangers around the distant planet called earth, would see him walking on the moon as the first child astronaut.

This time there was no fuzzy screen and no black and white images. Instead, Michael stared at high definition images of himself – the first child to make his way down a ladder and onto the surface of the moon. It looked as if it was meant to be. Even his voice sounded calm and almost like a proper astronaut. He was a proper astronaut.

The footage covered Michael and Buddy's first few minutes on the moon's surface and their first two collections of water-rich samples. Michael couldn't take his eyes off the screen as the two of them went about their work. Apart from their voices perhaps, there was nothing to give away their teenage status. All those years dreaming; the last eighteen months of training and Michael was starring in his very own moon landing film.

'So, Michael and Buddy,' said John Dell at the end of the video footage, ' in your own words, could you tell everyone watching at home what it was like up there.'

Michael and Buddy glanced at each other. Buddy was the one who always seemed most comfortable talking. He'd talk to almost anyone about almost anything and loved his life as an astronaut-in-the-making. He also seemed to know exactly what to say in any situation. Michael, on the other hand, was getting better, but no match for his confident friend.

Buddy nodded to Michael to go first.

'Er...hello, everyone. This is Michael May of *Explorer 4*,' he said, forcing a larger smile than usual, 'and member of the *Fortis* mission. Thank you for joining us on this really special day for the US, European and Russian space agencies.

He paused for a second. Just in front of the cameras, he had to forget about the sudden change in the *Fortis* mission objectives. He had to forget that one of the samples of PM4 had gone missing, that Jia Li had turned up pretending she was someone else and that Ralph and *Inceptor 1* had faced near-death experiences. And, he also had to leave out the most important part about Buddy and him almost being stranded on the moon.

'Er…I now know why previous astronauts hesitate when they're asked this,' said Michael, fumbling for the right words. 'It's one of those questions that's really hard to answer, but I'll do my best. It's a bit like waiting for Christmas when you're really young. You want it to be here so much that it seems to take forever. You've memorised your list, you know when it's going to happen, but time drags. Then suddenly you wake up and it's Christmas morning. You can't quite believe it, but when you check the clock and look around your room, you know the magic has happened. That's how today felt,' he said, sensing a ball of something restricting his throat. 'I've been waiting for this Christmas since I was really young and today it arrived.'

Michael's voice wavered.

Buddy smiled at him and nodded in encouragement.

'None of us really knew what to expect,' continued Michael. 'I mean we've all seen the Apollo landings on the near side, but we're the first to get this close to the far side and it's so totally different. I suppose I was taken aback by the size of the craters and mountains. You read about something over a mile wide, but it doesn't mean much until you actually see it for yourself.'

Michael raised his eyebrows at Buddy.

'Hi, this is Buddy Russell. Thanks for tuning in today to follow our awesome landing on the moon. I think Mike summed it up perfectly. It's a dream come true; in fact, for me, it's several dreams come true. Like Mike, I've always stared up at our silvery friend and wondered, I've always followed astronauts and how they've pushed the boundaries of space exploration and I can't believe I've had the chance to see it for real.'

He beamed one of his good-looking, charming smiles at the screen and pushed back his hair. 'I just want to thank everyone for giving us this opportunity, for Bob Sturton's training, which was fair but wasn't always easy, to the *Fortis* mission crew for helping us when things got tough...' He paused and turned to Michael. '...And to my best friend, Mike, for being there when I needed him most.'

There were more cheers from Mission Control as Steve gave Michael and Buddy big, friendly slaps on the back.

'And what about you, Marat?' asked John Dell. 'How was it piloting *Explorer 4* but not getting to walk on the moon?'

Michael looked at the stern-faced man and prayed that he could say something positive to the billions watching them.

'I am honoured to represent ROSCOSMOS and the European Space Agency on this historic return to the moon. From an operational perspective, the mission went well,' said Marat, betraying not a single emotion in his voice.

'That's great, Marat, but for the people watching right now, could you tell us how it felt?' said John Dell.

It was as if someone had asked Marat to give the value of pi to fifty decimal places. He looked bemused, unsure and completely uncomfortable.

'It was...it was a very special mission and as I said, it made me proud to be involved in such an important and historic event,' said Marat, shifting in his seat. 'I was more than content to be the one to pilot us down and back from the moon. I do not seek fame or glory for the work I do.'

Marat was just priceless. He'd had a chance to excite the world; to talk about the glorious sights they'd been privileged to see and all he could come up with was 'I was more than content'.

John Dell finished their live broadcast by talking to Steve about the meteoroid storm they'd survived. Michael smiled at Steve's description. He made it sound like he'd had to navigate through some rush hour traffic, rather than avoid a cataclysmic collision with supercharged rocks.

Michael didn't know whether to be impressed with everyone's casual comments or annoyed at the number of 'events' or 'happenings' that seemed to have been swept under the carpet. As Steve pressed the communication button to end the broadcast, Michael decided he'd had enough of keeping quiet. He was going find out what Jia Li (or whatever she was calling herself now) was really doing on the ISS and prove she'd stolen the PM4 sample.

With the broadcast over, the crew now had the relatively simple task of breaking free from the moon's orbit and returning to the ISS – assuming there were no rogue meteoroids this time. Steve checked their coordinates and angle of inclination and they put on their helmets and gloves.

'Systems and pressure nominal,' said Marat. 'Leak checks complete.'

'Looks like we're ready to go home,' said Steve. 'Crew to standby.'

Home, thought Michael…where was home these days? He'd moved from Andoverford in England to Florida more than two years ago. Then he'd had stays in Russia and Germany as part of his training. A few days ago he'd been fired up to a maze of tunnels and compartments called the ISS and now he was returning there from a trip to the moon.

'Launch sequence initiated,' said Steve.

Michael buried his head in his headrest and waited for the almost familiar ten-second countdown.

'And ten…nine…eight…'

This might be the last time he'd be in the moon's orbit. There were no guarantees in space travel and plans were easily changed or scrapped. His notebooks were full of stories of men and women who'd never quite made it into space. Bob Sturton and Ralph were just two examples. He said a long goodbye in his head and thanked the moon for showing him some mercy when things had become really serious.

'Three…two…one…we have engine ignition and…'

Before Steve could finish his sentence, Michael felt a boot in his back and he was immediately pinned to his seat.

'Crew status?' asked Steve.

'Nominal,' replied Buddy, 'but it feels like my mom's just jumped on me.'

Michael would have laughed if he'd been able to get enough air into his lungs.

The excitement and anticipation that had accompanied Michael on his journey to the moon were replaced by a very different feeling on the way back. He couldn't get the picture of Jia Li waving from the *Cupola* out of his head. How had she been allowed to come up with the Chinese crew after being thrown off the CMP for sabotaging the others? Surely she wasn't the right person to be representing her country and why had she replaced the astronaut they'd seen at the Chinese press conference only a few months ago? Dread…that was what Michael felt now…a feeling of dread at having to confront her in a little less than twelve hours' time.

'Reducing thrust to eighty per cent,' said Steve, suddenly. 'It should be much easier for you all now. Perhaps you ought to try and get some rest.'

Michael doubted he'd be able to rest with countless thoughts tumble-drying in his head. He stared at what Bob Sturton had called the 'visual impression experienced when no visible light reaches the eye' (his description of black) but, as he tried to get his eyes to focus on something out of his window, his eyelids decided he'd seen enough. They rolled down like shop door shutters and there was not a thing he could do about it.

Chapter Sixteen

Michael had to do a double take at his watch to believe that he'd slept for five hours.

'Don't worry, dude,' said a cheerful Buddy beside him, 'I covered your leak checks and cabin pressure.'

'Er...thanks,' said Michael, 'I'm not sure what happened there. I just...'

'Just fell asleep so heavily that I started to wish I had a giant marker pen on me.'

'What?'

'...To draw on your face, of course. I think you'd suit a curly moustache and bushy eyebrows.'

After what they'd been through...after what Buddy had been through, how could he make jokes? Michael wished he had a bit more of Buddy in him.

'D'you feel better now?' asked Steve.

'Yes, thanks. Much better,' said Michael tipping his neck from side to side.

'That was one long day,' said Steve, blowing out his cheeks and rubbing his face. 'At least I got to doze for a few minutes at a time when I was waiting for you.'

'Did you feel lonely?'

'Not really. The silence was a bit odd, but then I got used to it and, with only me on board, I was quite busy. I had to check my orbit coordinates, panel readouts and keep track of your timescales. What about you? I know what you said to the camera earlier, but how was it...really? You don't look like I thought you would. I imagined you'd be raving about it, unable to stop talking about the most memorable trip of your life.'

Michael hesitated. What should he say? Marat was only half a metre away and even though he appeared to be sleeping, he might not be. Should he even care what Marat thought? The whole crew would soon find out about their close shave on the moon and they'd have to investigate.

'No, you're right, Steve,' said Michael eventually. 'It was the most amazing trip of my life.'

'Then why the face?'

'Er...I didn't know I was pulling one.'

'What happened?'

'What d'you mean?' said Michael, now fiddling with an imaginary piece of something on the edge of his seat.

'You were the first child to go into space, the first to walk on the moon, you've collected the samples you were asked to collect and got back safely to rendezvous with me on *Inceptor 1*. You've had something to eat and a five-hour sleep, yet you look like someone's died. You don't have to tell me what's up, Michael, but it might help if you did.'

'Er...I do want to talk to you,' Michael said, glancing over at a still Marat. 'It's just that I'm really tired and would prefer to do it when we get back to the ISS.'

'That's not a problem,' said Steve, turning back to his screen. 'Whenever you're ready, just come and find me.'

Michael nodded. All he had to do now was to work out how he was going to tell Steve the whole story about Jia Li and the other stuff, without sounding like a paranoid, tell-tale kid.

Five hours was most of a school day, thought Michael, as he waited for Steve to announce the docking sequence with the ISS. He would have had six lessons, played football and had his dinner in that time. Instead, he'd been gazing out of a small window at the blackest black he'd ever seen, thinking about what he'd have to face when he got back.

Bang! Michael's thoughts were immediately fractured by a noise, followed by a violent shudder.

'Booster rockets jettisoned,' said Marat. 'Burns to commence in thirty seconds.'

Michael had totally forgotten that they needed to get rid of the *Exploration Return Stage* booster rockets before docking. He'd been daydreaming and needed to start concentrating again. He'd be straight back to his work schedule as soon as he got on board the ISS.

Inserting *Inceptor 1* back into the ISS orbit was a full-on job for Marat and Steve. It was every bit as difficult as their first arrival at the ISS, even more so after a long mission to the moon and very little sleep.

Michael felt each successive nudge as the burns got them into the perfect position for docking. It was now in view and just the sight of it made his stomach ripple. Was it excitement at being back or was it panic at what lay ahead?

'Docking in approximately twenty minutes,' said Marat.

The ISS solar arrays sent a lightning flash of reflected sunlight.

'Nearly home,' said Buddy.

Michael smiled. He hadn't ever thought he'd be so glad to get back to this odd sci-fi-looking piece of junk.

The ISS docking port came into view on the black and white screen.

'Reduce speed. One metre,' said Steve. 'Fifty centimetres… and twenty…ten…five…and…docking *Inceptor 1* to the ISS.'

There was that slight clunk again as the two craft came into contact and although they'd done this before, Michael breathed out a slow, relieved breath.

'Mission Control, this is *Inceptor 1*,' said Steve. 'Docking procedure is complete. The probe is secure. Contact and capture.'

'Roger that, *Inceptor 1*. Well done guys,' said John Dell. 'That was some mission.'

'Prepare for disembarkation.' Steve clapped his hands

together and pulled himself along the ceiling towards the hatch door.

Michael prayed it would be Ru, Shen, Sarah or Ralph on the other side. In fact, he'd be happy to see anyone other than that cheat, Jia Li.

The traditional knocking began on both sides of the hatch and, far quicker than the first time, the handle rotated through a hundred and eighty degrees. The suction on the hatch door was broken and a wisp of blond hair floated in.

'So how was our favourite satellite, then?' said Sarah, with a face-engulfing smile and saucer-sized eyes. 'Welcome home, guys. You did it. You took a spacecraft back up to the moon and got to see the far side. Was it amazing? Was it just the most beautiful, awesome sight you've ever seen?'

The words spurted out of her mouth like a volcano erupting.

Maybe he wasn't important in all of this, thought Michael. Maybe others saw things so differently that he should allow them their excitement. They'd just achieved something huge – a mission that might not be repeated for a long time. Maybe he should enjoy the celebrations before he brought people down with his suspicions and accusations?

'D'you want to let us get out of here first before we tell you all about it, Sarah?' said Steve, still smiling.

'Oops. Sorry. Just really excited for you guys,' she said, reversing to let them out.

Michael was next to leave *Inceptor 1*, pulling his bag, helmet and gloves with him. Suddenly a flash blinded him. He turned his head to avoid it, bumping into the side of the chamber.

A snort erupted from behind.

'Never been that good with the paparazzi have you,

Mike.' Buddy pushed past and fiddled with his hair. 'Just go with it and you might actually enjoy yourself,' he said, flashing a row of straight teeth at Sarah as she took more photos of the returning heroes.

Michael gave Sarah the pictures she wanted and the pictures he knew his family would want to see – a smiling teenager with his thumbs up, returning safely from a historic mission to the moon.

'Welcome back to the ISS, guys,' said Ralph, his hand still bandaged and now in a cloth sling, clipped to his belt. 'You did an awesome job. Come and get something to eat and drink and then you can brief us about what you found.'

'What about the samples?' asked Michael. 'D'you want us to get them?' Surely they shouldn't leave them just a hatch away from whoever had stolen the PM4 sample.

'They can stay there for now,' said Ralph with a look that told Michael not to worry. 'They're all sealed and weighed. We'll go down later and get them. You just sort yourself out first.'

Ralph was right. There were three things Michael was desperate for now he was back on the ISS. The first was food – he didn't care what it was or what it tasted like; he just needed to reintroduce his stomach to something solid and filling. The gooey stuff he'd squeezed into his mouth over the past day and a half had kept him going, but he just wanted that feeling of being full and satisfied. The second was a shower. He knew that was a physical impossibility, but a proper wash would be great. None of them could smell that good after such a long time in a spacesuit. Finally, he wanted to call home and speak to his family. After hearing about Buddy's mum and dad and the problems he'd had to deal with, he just needed to hear their voices.

'Greetings to our heroes from *Inceptor 1*,' said Ru, as

Michael arrived in the galley. 'We hope you will accept our hospitality as we provide you with a celebratory meal,' he said, pointing to a variety of yellow-tabbed pouches and containers attached to the table.

He'd rather have eaten with the *Fortis* crew. He needed to talk to them about what had happened to Ralph, to the PM4 samples and to Buddy on the moon. He also had to tell them about Yue Shi and who she really was.

Within minutes, Ru, Shen and the entire *Fortis* crew gathered around the table. Unfortunately, so did Jia Li.

Michael picked up on the odd atmosphere. Those who'd stayed on the ISS were celebrating an exciting, groundbreaking and successful mission, the astronauts who'd just returned looked like deflated tyres and the Chinese team couldn't stop asking questions.

'How did the surface of the moon appear, Michael?' asked Shen, raising his dark, perfectly semi-circular eyebrows.

'How many kilos of water-rich soil did you retrieve?' asked Ru.

'You did a good job,' said Yue, almost under her breath.

Michael wasn't sure if she was being nice or sarcastic. He and Buddy turned up just the slightest corner of their mouths but said nothing.

'I think, guys,' said Ralph, 'these folks just need to eat first and then answer questions later. It's got to be one of the most exhausting missions so far and they look like they need a few minutes.'

Meatballs in a rich tomato sauce with pasta had never tasted so good and Michael was soon reaching for another pouch.

'I'd never really appreciated these babies before,' said Buddy, wiping a meandering trickle of sauce from his chin. 'This is a banquet, Ru. Thanks.'

'We need to celebrate a day like this,' said Ru, patting Buddy on the back. 'That two children train to come into space is amazing; for those two children to successfully complete a mission to the moon is exceptional. I hope you do not mind if I take a photograph of you both to send to Chinese Mission Control. They will be celebrating too when they see your faces.'

Michael stopped chewing. He'd had thousands of photos taken of him since winning a place on the CMP. He reckoned he'd got much better at smiling on cue but, with Yue standing right behind Ru as he lifted the camera, he was put off...put off smiling...almost put off eating. She looked the same cold, sinister person he knew from before, but with a new, unnerving confidence.

Ru didn't seem to notice and clicked away until he got what he wanted.

Buddy was straight back to his food – dessert this time. 'Mm...pecan pie,' he mumbled through his hamster cheeks. 'You gotta taste this to believe it, dude.'

Michael savoured the same rush of sugar and comfort as he rolled the sticky, warm goo around his mouth. He was immediately back at home at Sunday lunch with his family. His dad had just piled his plate high with roast chicken, his mum was dashing back and forwards from the kitchen to check the progress of the apple pie and Millie was recounting her last drama at school. This was almost the only time they all sat together to eat and even then, it was only one in every two or three weekends that Michael could get home from his training. It was their only opportunity to download what they'd been up to and what they'd be doing the following week. He loved it.

Since moving to Florida, his dad had recovered fully from his accident and although covered with scars and pit marks where the pins had been, his leg was pretty much back to normal – enough to kick a football around and try to outjump him at basketball. He still worked long hours, but always made it to Michael's press conferences and never worked at weekends. His mum had also changed since the accident. She seemed more relaxed, less anxious and actually looked like she was enjoying her time with them. This was so different from life in Andoverford. All of it was so different.

As Michael slurped the last dregs of mood-altering dessert he thought about his granny. Even though she'd celebrated her eightieth birthday the year before, she still came over to Florida every few months, booking her own seats online and travelling alone. 'As long as I have a good magazine, my glasses and my humbugs, I'll be alright,' she always said.

'So, are you going to do it now, Buddy?' said Michael, finishing Ru's banquet with a strawberry milkshake drink.

'Do what now?' asked Buddy, stuffing his empty pouches into the waste bag.

'Try and find your dad,' said Michael.

Buddy didn't move.

'Buddy?'

'Yeah. I heard you the first time, Mike,' snapped Buddy. 'I said I'd do it, didn't I.'

Michael left it and turned away to sort out the second on his 'to do' list.

'And what about you, Mike?' said Buddy from behind. 'You said you were going to speak to Ralph and Steve and get to the bottom of all the stuff that's happened since we've been up here.'

'I *am* going to,' said Michael, feeling his stomach tense at the thought, 'but I can't speak to Ralph smelling like this.' He lifted up his right arm and pretended to sniff underneath.

'That's gross, man! I'm outta here.'

He'd never really craved a shower before now, in fact, his parents always had to 'encourage' him to have one at home but, just this second Michael, would have traded almost anything to have been standing in a shower with jets of hot water massaging his back. He looked in the mirror at a dirty, exhausted and worried face and even after he'd squeezed some water onto a cloth and removed the grey smudges across his face, the worry remained.

'Now *you* look better,' said Steve, when Michael appeared nearly an hour later. 'Sometimes it's just nice to be somewhere where you can't be seen, isn't it? It can get a bit overwhelming.'

Michael nodded, turning his head away so Steve couldn't see him clenching his jaw.

'Do you fancy helping me with the mission report? I've just got to enter my activities, readings and logs and then we can do yours.'

Michael pulled himself along to the side of the module where several laptops were secured and looked at what Steve had written so far. The first part read like a sci-fi horror story, with the meteoroid storm described in huge detail. The hairs on Michael's forearms tingled as he thought back to the mechanical, yet panicked few minutes they'd experienced. Steve's report included information like the time of the storm, the coordinates given by John Dell at Mission Control, as well as a transcript of what had been said on board *Inceptor 1*. Michael had to read the next part of the report twice to make sure he understood. Steve had set out the details of his time from entering the moon's orbit to leaving it. But there was no description of what they'd seen and done and how amazing this had been, just a factual recount of the procedures they'd followed and the data they'd captured. He didn't get it.

'I know what you're thinking,' said Steve, without looking at Michael. 'Sounds like the instructions for a washing machine or the map coordinates for a family holiday in the hills, doesn't it? We have to write a purely factual report on what we did and what we saw – nothing more. It's a bit boring, to be honest...there we go. That's my bit done. D'you want to get yours done while I'm here?'

Michael hesitated. He knew he'd have to talk to Steve eventually. If he did it now, maybe Steve would talk to Ralph. Maybe he could be the one to tell the crew that, not only did they have a thief and a saboteur on board, but that they had someone here with a fake name, who'd already been prepared to kill to get what she wanted.

Chapter Seventeen

'If you think about it, it makes perfect sense.'

'Now hold on a minute, Michael,' said Steve, lowering his voice. 'I know you think there's something going on and you could be right. But you can't make these sorts of accusations without some evidence.'

'Jia Li, as she was called back then, deliberately sabotaged three people, that we know about, on the CMP. Aiko nearly suffocated because of her, Matthaeus failed the swim because she rubbed a chest ointment on the inside of his goggles and she put laxatives in Liam's food. She even locked me in a wardrobe! What kind of normal person does this? She gets kicked off the programme and then turns up two years later on the ISS with a new name.' The heat spread across Michael's cheeks and he swallowed. She wasn't going to get away with it. He was going to make sure of that.

'I'd no idea,' said Steve in a softer tone. 'How did she manage to convince the Chinese Space Agency?'

'I don't know. Maybe the whole Chinese Space Agency's in on it.'

'Tell me the other stuff you think's been happening again, Michael...but slowly this time.'

Michael ran through his suspicions about the missing PM4 sample, the unlikelihood that what happened to Ralph was due to equipment failure and the malfunction of Buddy's carbon dioxide removal system. 'Even if Ralph's accident really *was* an accident,' said Michael, speeding up, 'and something weird had gone wrong with Buddy's CO2 system in between leaving here and getting to the moon, you still can't explain where the missing PM4 sample is, can you?'

Steve rubbed his face with both palms. Michael hadn't seen him like this before. This was a man who'd spent years as an RAF jet fighter, who'd played a part in more conflicts than Michael had even heard about and was used to making split-second decisions about really serious stuff. Now he looked like a man who couldn't even decide which flavour ice cream to have.

'We should tell Ralph and the others immediately. This is too serious to keep to ourselves,' said Steve.

'That's what I thought before, but if we tell everyone, won't the person or people responsible start being extra careful? Then we might never find out who's to blame.'

'So, what do you suggest?'

'Er…well we all know about the PM4 test tube and that what happened to Ralph was probably not an accident, but for now only you, me and Buddy know about Jia Li. We've got our mission debrief later, so why don't we see if we can find out anything before then.'

'OK, Michael. Let's try that first but, whatever happens, we tell the rest of the team at our debrief. Now, do you want to get your report done before I pass it on to Marat?'

Now there was a name that gave Michael an uneasy feeling. It was like Marat didn't really want to be here, didn't like anyone and was determined to make things difficult for others. And Michael just couldn't make sense of the fact that Marat had moved *Vader* in the opposite direction to him and Buddy.

Now that he knew what his report should contain, writing it was fairly easy. He needed to document the bare facts about following his instructions on *Inceptor 1*, *Vader* and the moon. He did mention the trouble with the *Speeder* to account for him and Buddy being late back to their pick-up point and the problems with Buddy's CO2 removal system but he kept it to the facts, as he knew them.

Once he'd finished, he logged off, closed the laptop lid and pushed himself off the side of the *Destiny* lab wall. He'd just have time to do his air contamination and carbon dioxide removal checks, call his parents and have a quick snoop around before meeting the rest of the *Fortis* crew for their debrief.

Inside his sleep station, Michael suddenly had an urge to put on his sleeping bag cocoon, forget about everything and stay there for the rest of the day.

'Knock, knock,' said a voice from the other side of his flimsy door.

'Come in,' said Michael, 'I mean, don't come in. There isn't enough room for two…oh, you know what I mean.'

'Are you OK?' asked Buddy.

'Yeah, just tired and a bit…'

'Fed up? Shaken?'

'Yeah, both of those,' said Michael, not even noticing Buddy's crumpled face.

'What are you doing now?'

'I'm going to call my parents and let them know I'm…' He wanted to say, 'let them know I'm fine,' but wasn't sure whether the words and his face would say the same thing. 'Er…I'm just going to talk to them and let them know that I'm back safely. Then I'm going to have a look around to see if I can work out what's been going on. I've talked to Steve and he's going to give me until our debrief before we tell everyone about Jia Li and the other stuff.'

Buddy didn't respond, so Michael grabbed the rim of the sleep station entrance and pulled his head down and out.

'Are you OK?' asked Michael, noticing Buddy's puffy eyes.

Buddy's jaw was clenched tight and he shook his head.

'What's happened? Have you found something?'

Buddy shook his head again.

Michael suddenly got it – there weren't many things that made Buddy lose his wide smile and sense of fun. 'Er...I take it you spoke to your dad then and it didn't go too well,' he said, wishing he was better at these sorts of things. 'Well at least you tried, and you won't keep on wondering. I mean, at least he knows you're interested, even if he's not. Sorry it's not better news.'

Buddy was still shaking his head, but Michael had run out of words. He didn't know whether to pat Buddy on the back or leave him alone.

Buddy whispered something too quietly for Michael to catch.

'What did you say?'

'It was brilliant,' said Buddy, looking up at Michael with a face that hadn't yet caught up with his words.

'Brilliant? What was?'

'Talking to my dad. I talked to my dad and it was brilliant.'

Michael waited for more, but Buddy was clearly reliving the conversation in his head, rather than out loud. 'And?'

'I managed to track him down online. Anyway, I decided not to send him an email, but call him. It's still afternoon there and I had to get it over with...and he answered. Can you believe it? It was actually him who answered.'

'And how was it? I mean was it really weird talking to him after all that time?'

'Actually, it wasn't weird. It was kinda easy. Once he'd got over the shock of me calling him, I couldn't stop him talking. He knows everything I've been up to since getting on the CMP. He's kept every newspaper clipping and recorded every interview and piece of TV footage with me on it. It was amazing, Mike...really amazing.'

'Er...and did you ask why he...'

'Left?'

Michael nodded.

'All I know is that it wasn't anything to do with me and that's good enough. It was something that went on between Mom and Dad and he said that he shouldn't have let it affect our relationship.'

'So, what now?'

'That's the best bit,' said Buddy, like an over-excited five-year-old. 'He wants to come and see me when we get back from our mission. He wants to be there when we land.'

'Wow! That's great news, but how's your mum going to react?'

Buddy's face immediately lost its sparkle.

'Hey, I'm sorry, Buddy. I didn't mean to...'

'Don't worry. I'm going to have to tell her that I talked to my dad and then break the news that he'll be there when we get back. What can she do? She can't stop me from seeing him.'

'Mm, that's true, but you might need to break it to her a little more gently than that, Buddy. She's had you all to herself all this time – it's going to be a shock for her and you know how your mum deals with shock.'

'You're right. I'll speak to her soon and tell her. She'll have a few weeks to get used to the idea, then.'

'I'm really happy for you, Buddy,' said Michael, giving his friend a pat on the shoulder.

Michael smiled as Buddy left. Once he'd spoken to his parents, it'd be his turn to do something difficult.

It was Granny May who answered.

'It's me, Granny,' said Michael, grinning at her amazing ability to forget everything she'd ever been told about how to 'video call' someone.

'Michael, my dear!' warbled his granny. 'How are you?'

'It's OK. You don't have to talk loudly or slowly. I can hear you perfectly well.'

'Are you still on the moon?' she asked, ignoring the sleeping bag floating directly behind him and the pictures of his mum and dad on the wall.

'No, I'm back on the ISS now. We got back a couple of hours ago. I've just had something to eat and a wash, so I thought I'd give you a quick call to let you know that I'm fine.'

'We were so worried for you, Michael,' said his granny, stroking her pearl necklace and patting the side of her hair in the screen reflection. 'Was it really frightening?'

Michael wasn't sure how to answer. Surviving a meteoroid storm and being stranded on the moon with his best friend in real trouble had all been terrifying, but he couldn't exactly tell his granny that. 'Er...it was an experience I won't ever forget,' he said, truthfully.

'Is that my boy?' came a booming voice from behind his granny. 'Just tell me that it was the most amazing, heart-stoppingly beautiful place you've ever seen,' said Michael's dad, rubbing his hands together in excitement. 'Was it? Was it just everything we talked about?'

Michael smiled at the boyish face that now took up the whole of the screen as he pressed it up close to the camera. 'Yes, Dad, it was everything we talked about...and more. The colours were even more diverse than we reckoned, the difference between the tallest mountains and the deepest craters was completely unbelievable and the view of the earth was exactly like the posters, but better!' Michael could have talked all night to his dad like this. Apart from Buddy and Steve, his dad was the person who understood best what being here meant to him.

'What was the walking like? You looked brilliant...no stumbles and what you said made us all...' His dad didn't finish his sentence, stopping instead to wipe the normal-looking water from his eyes.

'Thanks. Is Mum there?'

'Yes, she's by my side, listening to everything. Viv, Michael wants to see you.'

'Hi, Michael,' said his mum, using her 'smiling-but-secretly-relieved' look. 'Well done, love. We're all so proud of you. Millie's been telling the whole world about you and can't wait to show you off to her friends and Dad and I can't really believe what you've done. You've worked so hard for this and at last, it's come true for you. We just couldn't be happier.'

Michael smiled back. He knew that she'd really be a lot happier if he was sitting right next to her or slumped on the couch playing on his games console, but he felt better just seeing her and listening to her voice.

'Hey, Michael, we're going to wave to you tonight!' said his dad. 'You're going overhead in about ten and a half hours according to my ISS App,' he said, holding his phone up to the screen.

'I'll make sure I wave then,' said Michael, smiling at the thought of his dad having to find the fast, bright arc of light in the sky and convince granny May that her grandson was on board. 'I see you've put on one of your favourite shirts as a treat for me.' He had no idea why, but his dad seemed to have a love for hideous, Hawaiian-type shapeless shirts and could produce one to embarrass him on almost every occasion.

Suddenly his parents disappeared. He'd lost the connection. He dialled again, but there was no answer. They'd probably travelled out of satellite range – one of the hazards of racing along at 17,500 miles an hour. Still, at least he'd seen his family and they knew he was OK.

Before leaving his sleep station he fired off two emails,

both on his private account. One was to Charlotte, his girlfriend at home. He didn't know how things were going to work out with them living on different continents. They'd seen each other a few times since he'd moved to Florida and she was coming out to see him for the first time eight weeks after his return.

'Hey, Mike. Come on. Hurry up,' said Buddy's voice from outside Michael's sleep station.

'I know, I know. We've only got half an hour until our debrief,' said Michael, pressing the send button on his second email to Jamie.

'I don't mean that,' said Buddy, panting like a dog.

'Have you been exercising? I didn't think you were doing that until later?'

'No, I'm not, but I just need to you come with me right now and don't ask stupid questions!' Buddy turned and pushed off the wall.

With only the robotic humming of the ISS for sound, they silently made their way to the *Dàdǎn* module.

'Look!' said Buddy, as they entered the pristine Chinese module with its state-of-the-art design and equipment.

'At what?' Michael scanned the empty module.

'Exactly! There's no one here. Ru and Shen are doing their EVA to finish the Chinese airlock,' said Buddy, looking like he'd won the jackpot. 'And Jia Li is operating the SSRMS. We've got the place to ourselves. Now's our chance to see what we can find.'

Chapter Eighteen

Michael and Buddy worked their way from one end of the *Dàdǎn* module to the other, opening drawers, looking in the MSG and checking every bottle, bag and container they came across.

'Make sure you put everything back exactly as it is,' said Michael. 'We don't want anyone complaining that we're spying on them before we've got something concrete.' He should be having a bit of relaxation before their debrief; instead, he was looking for evidence of stealing, sabotage and probably worse...all in a confined space, two hundred and forty miles above the earth.

'Got anything, Mike?' said Buddy, upside down, looking behind the casing of one of the air filters.

'Nothing...you?'

'No...just an air filter that could do with cleaning out.'

'Let's have a quick look at the sleep stations and then we'll have to go,' said Michael, bubbles of panic rising in his stomach. If they couldn't find anything, he'd look like some stupid kid who'd watched too many crime dramas.

'Right, let's check two each. You take Jia Li and Ru's. I'll take Shen and Marat's,' said Buddy, already slotting his feet into the first, like he was loading a shell into a gun.

The wedge-shaped sleep stations had just enough room for Michael to turn upside down and around 360 degrees. Ru's sleep station was tidy and sparsely decorated, like most of them. There were two photos of some sort of celebration stuck to one wall. Ru and Shen were in their flight suits shaking hands with a serious-faced, suited man. With a large Chinese flag behind them, Michael guessed it was the day when they'd been announced as the first Chinese crew to visit the ISS. On the other wall were Ru's timetable, a picture of his parents, a book and a miniature Chinese flag.

Michael lifted the lid on Ru's laptop, but it was turned off. Next, he flicked through the first few pages of the book. Although it was written in Chinese, there were pictures of spacecraft and flight trajectories, so Michael guessed it was something to do with their mission or the history of Chinese space travel.

'You found anything, Mike?' called Buddy from next door.

'Nothing at all. You?'

'Only that Shen has a secret stash of Chinese comics and boiled sweets in here. Do you think he'd miss one?'

Just entering Jia Li's sleep station made Michael feel uneasy. He remembered her room at the CMP – perfectly ordered and so tidy that it felt like an adult's room rather than a teenager's. There were no pictures on the wall here and the only book Michael found was something science-related. He scanned the pages of intricate Chinese characters, but it meant nothing to him. He was about to close it when he noticed what Jia Li had been using as a bookmark. It was a photograph of two Chinese men in suits...in what had to be a hospital. He turned it over and studied the neat line of handwritten characters. If only he could read Chinese.

Next, he searched Jia Li's clothes. It felt wrong, but he only had one chance and he wasn't about to waste it. There was only her sleeping bag left, attached by a small loop of fabric to a ring on the wall. He patted it down from the hood to the bottom; assuming that the lump in the base was her night clothes. He squeezed to check that there was nothing else there but the lump felt like more than just clothes. It was bulkier and had a very definite shape. He unzipped the sleeping bag and pushed his arm to the bottom. 'I don't believe it! You thieving little...'

But his insult was cut short by the sudden arrival of arguing voices.

He put back Jia Li's sleep station as best he could, stuffed his discovery down his t-shirt then dived straight out and into the adjacent one – right on top of Buddy.

'Hey, man!' said Buddy, pushing Michael away. 'What are you...?'

Michael slammed his forefinger across his lips before jabbing it towards the mouth of the sleep station.

The boys hovered next to each other, as the confrontation volume increased.

The voices were definitely Chinese, and Michael immediately recognised the loudest as Jia Li's. But he couldn't tell if the other voice was Ru or Shen's. He edged as close to the curtain as he dared and peered through the gap. He could see Jia Li waving her arms around, hissing like a venomous snake. Someone had made her really mad. He still couldn't see who she was shouting at until the conversation ended abruptly and Marat glided straight past the sleep station and out of the *Dàdǎn* module.

'It's Marat,' Michael mouthed silently to Buddy. 'Jia Li and Marat.'

Michael looked at his watch. They were due to meet the rest of the *Fortis* crew in five minutes, but he couldn't be sure whether Jia Li was still outside or not. He counted to sixty in his head and signalled to Buddy. Then they slid out of the sleep station and around the corner like silent eels, not stopping until they were back in the *Destiny* module.

'What was that all about?' asked Buddy, looking like he'd just taken part in an adrenalin-fuelled car chase. 'Might have been useful if we'd learned Chinese too.'

Michael nodded. Why had Jia Li been arguing with Marat? He didn't think they knew each other well enough to be arguing about anything. And what had been the point of taking Cyril, their mascot?

'So, I've read through your reports and, apart from a violent meteoroid storm that we threw in to challenge you, it looks like it was pretty much a textbook landing and successful moon mission,' said Ralph.

This was the moment, thought Michael. This was the time when everything would come out...all the coincidences, the accidents and unexplained events. He looked at Steve, then to Marat.

'In my role as *Vader* pilot,' said Marat, 'it was a successful landing, sample collection and rendezvous with *Inceptor 1*. We did have a small problem with a CO_2 removal system malfunction in Buddy's suit, but he wasn't compromised. Buddy and Michael struggled to operate the *Speeder*, delaying their return, but we were still successful in meeting our rendezvous schedule. The full complement of samples was harvested and our lunar mapping photographs were completed.'

It was Steve's turn next and to Michael's horror, he gave the same sort of methodical report as Marat, describing the meteoroid storm and showing the rest of the crew the footage he'd captured of the moon from *Inceptor 1*.

It was stunning and Michael could have stared at the silvery-grey surface with its peaks and troughs for hours... just not now. 'Er...excuse me, Ralph,' he said, forcing his eyes to look up. 'I know this is very important, but I think you'll find that it's all covered in our reports. The thing is, we haven't really done anything about the missing PM4 sample or the malfunctioning SSRMS and there are a couple of other things that I'd like to mention about our far side mission.' He knew that his face had coloured but didn't care.

'I agree,' said Steve, quickly. 'Michael and I talked about it at length and we can't have experiment samples going missing. Also, when we checked the SSRMS earlier, it was working perfectly from both robotic workstations. That means someone was overriding the boys' controls in the *Cupola* and that means that your injury wasn't accidental, Ralph.'

Ralph nodded. 'It's one of the worst situations to be in,' he said, without his usual sparkle, 'and I'm going to have to notify Mission Control...not about the PM4, but about the SSRMS.'

Sarah, who'd been quiet throughout, suddenly pushed away from the table. 'This is ridiculous! We're not talking about someone losing a pair of socks. We're talking about someone stealing a potentially lethal sample for their own gain and we also know that it must be one of the nine of us on the ISS. That narrows it down a bit, doesn't it?'

'If we have nothing to hide, then why don't we search each other's sleep stations and equipment?' said Marat, calmly. 'That way we can say we've looked everywhere.'

Ralph nodded slowly, searching for the reaction in everyone else's face. There was more nodding around the table. 'OK, then. I'm going to go and see Ru, Shen and Yue and tactfully ask to do the same,' he said. 'Are you happy with that as a starting point, Michael?'

What should he say? He should have left Cyril in Jia Li's sleep station for someone else to find. He needed to show what kind of devious mind she possessed.

'Er...actually, Ralph, I need to tell you something about Yue,' said Michael.

'About me?' said a clipped voice from behind them. 'How kind that you are talking about me, Michael,' said Jia Li with a smile that Michael knew was completely fake. 'Are you telling the *Fortis* crew about my study on the Shenzhou programme and how I am the most highly qualified astronaut on it at only fifteen-years-old? Or perhaps you are explaining the book that I will be releasing, following my medical experiments on board the ISS?'

Michael froze, unable to get the slowly forming words out of his mouth fast enough.

Fortunately for Michael, Buddy didn't have the same problem. 'No, I think that what Mike was about to tell everyone is how you're not really called Yue Shi, but really Jia Li and that everything about you is phoney. You've probably changed your name because Jia Li was disqualified from the Children's Moon Program for cheating...for sabotaging the other children as part of a plan by her sponsors, who were paying for her training.' Buddy looked at the startled faces around the table. 'I also think that Mike was probably going to tell everyone that you would be our number one suspect for anything that goes wrong around here, that we don't trust or even like you and that we were horrified to see you taking a real astronaut's place up here.'

Jia Li's face didn't alter one bit and a small seed of panic suddenly started to sprout in Michael's stomach. What if she denied everything or made out that they were just jealous of her? What if no one believed them?

What Jia Li did next was completely unexpected and something Michael had never ever seen her do. She started to cry.

Sarah immediately bounded over to comfort her, and Ralph fidgeted uncomfortably, straightening his bandage.

Michael shot a glance at Marat to see his reaction but there was none. For someone who was arguing with her so loudly before, he looked completely disinterested, if not a little bored by the whole thing.

'Now look, Yue,' said Ralph eventually. 'I don't know

what's gone on in the past or how these two know you, but after spending the last couple of years training with them, I know they wouldn't make something like this up. There must be some way we can sort this whole thing out?'

Jia Li, who hadn't shed an actual tear whilst crying, looked up and after a few sniffs, spoke. 'Some of what Buddy says is true,' she said, making Buddy's eyebrows rise to the very top of his forehead in surprise. 'My birth name is Jia Li and I did take part in the Children's Moon Program. But the rest of what they say is false. I was wrongly accused of those things and it has taken me this time to rebuild my life.'

Michael wanted to speak. To anyone else this rubbish could sound so plausible that they might actually believe it. They didn't know Jia Li the way he and Buddy did. They hadn't heard the way she'd spoken to him after Aiko's accident, telling him that he'd be next.

'How did you manage to get on the Chinese mission?' said Buddy, saying what Michael was thinking. 'I mean, who would trust you after you got kicked off the CMP?'

'The sponsors who helped me study to get on the Shenzhou programme still had faith in my ability to be the best astronaut in the world. They knew that I needed to be on this mission,' said Jia Li, in a voice lacking warmth or colour.

'You mean they wanted to protect their investment,' said Buddy. 'They were the ones paying for you on the CMP and they were the ones telling you to get rid of your competition so that you could get a ride up here, weren't they?'

Jia Li shook her long, shiny hair from side to side like a swishing, dark curtain.

'But you weren't the first-choice astronaut, were you?' said Michael. 'We saw someone else at the press conference planning to take part in your mission. What happened?'

Jia Li didn't hesitate for a second. 'He became ill two days before launch and I was the natural choice from the backup crew,' she said.

'That's nice and convenient for you,' snapped Buddy.

'Look, guys,' said Sarah, holding the palm of her hands up in a mock stop sign in between the boys and Jia Li, 'does it really matter what happened two years ago and who was right or wrong? The point is that the ISS community has welcomed China as an International partner and Yue, or whatever she used to be called, has been chosen by her own country to represent them in space. Surely, we have to respect their decision?'

'I agree,' said Ralph. 'Unless someone has some concrete evidence right now that Yue has done something wrong, we need to let this go. We've got to live together up here, and this sort of tension and mistrust just isn't good for anyone. Michael?'

Michael wanted to say so much. He wanted to shout. He wanted to beg the rest of his crewmembers not to trust Jia Li, but Ralph was right. Apart from finding Cyril in her sleep station, he didn't have a single bit of evidence that Jia Li was up to anything at all.

Chapter Nineteen

'What are we supposed to do now?' said Michael. 'We've already checked everywhere we can think of. It's useless.'

Buddy shrugged. 'I'm gonna start my exercise now so I can get a bit longer for dinner and then I think I'm done for the day, Mike. I might phone Mom and tell her about Dad. I don't want her turning up and seeing him there without some sort of warning.'

Michael nodded. Poor Buddy had all this to deal with and there he was, worrying about a missing test tube, a stolen cuddly toy and a load of random coincidences.

By the time he stopped for dinner, Michael needed some time to himself. There was no one in the galley so he warmed up his chicken and rice stew, grabbed a handful of caramel cookies and headed back to his sleep station. He just wanted to eat, relax and catch up on some emails.

Michael smiled when he saw that Charlotte had replied to his email. It was brilliant to be on the same time zone as England for a change. She'd be back from Andoverford High School, the school he'd have gone to if he'd stayed in England. He missed normal things sometimes…just being one of the crowd and not singled out as special. Bet Darren Fletcher is still causing trouble and Adam Painter is telling awful Buddy-like jokes, thought Michael as he clicked on the mouse.

Hi Michael (or Mike as you're sometimes called in the US papers!). Just thought I'd mail you B4 I get on with my deadly dull chemistry homework. Still can't believe I'm stuck here while you're doing your exciting astronaut thing! It's so totally not fair (although I'm not sure I could be stuck in a metal box, whizzing around the earth like you! What happens if you want to get away from people??) Not much news here apart from that Darren Fletcher's been expelled for smoking at school (not a surprise to any of us) and Chester Stanford's moving to Berlin with his dad's job. I'm hoping to get a holiday job at the Presholm Hair Salon. To be honest, I hate the idea of getting up early on Saturday mornings, but I need the cash to upgrade my phone. My stingy parents won't cough up! May get the odd free haircut – you never know. So how is life up there? Saw your moon landing on the news and couldn't believe that was you in that suit! It feels a bit weird that you're looking down on us every few hours. Mum says I ought to go out and spot the ISS going over us, but you'd only look like a small bright light and we can always email and video call. Miss our long Sunday morning chats when you're home and can't wait to see you when you're done with all that astronaut stuff. Proud of you. C xx

Next was a reply from Jamie, which he really wanted to read but, just as he was about to open it, someone coughed outside his sleep station.

'Sorry to disturb you, Michael,' said a serious-faced Ralph. 'I need to speak with you.'

Michael slid out of his sleep station. Something must have happened. Ralph didn't just look unhappy or tired... he looked shocked.

'I need to ask you something really important,' said Ralph, swallowing before meeting Michael's eyes for only a fleeting moment. 'Marat came to see me just now,' he said, pointing behind him.

Michael twisted around to see Marat hovering by the entrance to the *Destiny* module before his eyes darted back to Ralph. This was all a bit heavy-handed to come and ask a question, wasn't it?

'It's like this, Michael,' said Ralph, now almost staring at him. 'We've found the missing PM4 test tube.'

It was one of those surreal moments, thought Michael, where the words didn't match the face – like a voice that's been dubbed in a film. Surely Ralph should look relieved or even pleased that he'd been right about Jia Li. Even a 'thank you' would have been nice.

'What did she say about it?' asked Michael. 'I bet she denied the whole thing, didn't she? That's just the sort of thing I'd expect from her...the lying...'

'Stop,' said Ralph, grabbing Michael by the arm. 'It's not Jia Li. She's got nothing to do with this,' and he turned towards Marat, beckoning him to come forward.

Then Michael saw it. It was Cyril...the *Fortis* mission mascot. What was Marat doing with it?

'You know we've all been looking for the missing PM4 sample, Michael?' said Ralph, turning Cyril around in his hands. 'Well, we...I mean Marat found it in your sleep station.' He twisted the stuffed alligator until its white belly was showing, pushed the fingers of his uninjured hand into a slit and pulled out a test tube.

'But that's...how could that have got...I mean I've no idea...'

'Do you have something to say about this, Michael?' Marat suddenly asked. 'What is your response to being found guilty of stealing the test tube that you accused Yue of taking?' He hovered in mid-air, his arms crossed like an angry Dad.

'Michael?' said Ralph.

'It wasn't me,' whispered Michael, more to himself than anyone else. How could they even think he'd do something like this? 'I said it wasn't me! I wouldn't do something like that! But I know who did and I'm going to have it out with her!' he shouted, trying to push past Marat.

'I'm sorry, Michael,' said Ralph, 'but I can't let you do that I'm afraid.'

'Do what?'

'Leave unaccompanied.'

'What?'

'Look, I hate to say this, Michael, but until we get to the bottom of this, you'll have to be accompanied wherever you go.'

'You've got to be joking!' shouted Michael. 'You can't be serious?'

But Marat's look was enough to tell Michael that they were exactly that...that they seriously thought that the boy, who'd spent half his life dreaming about space, was interested in ruining it all to get hold of some stupid 'maybe' vaccine.

'So basically, dude, you're the first person ever to be grounded...in space?' said Buddy, nodding to Ralph that he could go. 'That's some going.'

'It's not a joke, you idiot.' Michael tried to close his sleep station curtain with Buddy's arm in the way. 'Just imagine how you'd feel if you were accused of stealing.'

'Yeah, but I know you didn't do it, Mike. I don't know why you're so stressed out. We'll prove that Jia Li did it and then everyone will have to say sorry, won't they?'

'Brilliant idea, Buddy! In the meantime, everyone goes around thinking I'm a liar and a cheat. Perfect. Why didn't I think of that?' If he'd been at home he'd have slammed his door and dived onto his bed, but that was impossible here and so annoying. The best he could do was thump his fist on his sleep station wall and let out a long, silent scream.

There was no point trying to work at the moment and he didn't want to watch a movie on his own, so he flicked through the rest of his personal emails and clicked on the one from Jamie.

Jamie was skateboard-mad and his email began with him raving about his weekend. He'd entered yet another competition and from what Michael could tell, it was going to be a big one. Then something odd caught Michael's eye. Jamie described some of his favourite moves, like *backside grabs* and *carves*. These were phrases Michael had grown accustomed to (but moves he'd never mastered despite hours of help from Jamie). Then he went on to write about trying to *bust* a new move called the *darkslide*. In itself that wasn't weird, but Michael noticed that he'd written and underlined the word four times.

He slid his cursor over the word and it changed from black to blue. He was right. 'Please don't let the signal drop,' Michael whispered, as the whirling icon teased him.

His click landed him on a skateboarding blogging site, where all sorts of strangely nicknamed people were showing off their most dangerous moves and tricks. He scanned down the page. There was nothing out of the ordinary until he saw the word *darkslide* again with the initials MAM next to it. It couldn't be…could it? They were his initials. A second click took him straight to a paragraph of text on an otherwise empty page.

It read: *Thanks for your message about the darkslide. It's a super difficult move, but not impossible. Look at the video to see how it's done. There is video footage of almost every move if you look in the right place. Also, it's vital to use your arms. It's amazing how useful they can be if you have them in the right place to start with. Good luck and stay safe! JM.*

Michael re-read the message and thumped the top of his head to try and jump-start it into working properly. This was Jamie's reply to his earlier email asking for help, but what did he mean about videos and arms. It was no use. It was too late; he was too upset after what had happened earlier and anyway, he was stuck in his stupid sleep station now until someone came to get him in the morning.

Michael had slept surprisingly well on the ISS…until

now. The events of the day played themselves out in his dream as a mutant octopus kidnapped members of the *Fortis* crew, taking them out of the ISS. There, it waved them around with its slimy, green tentacles as they mouthed silent, tortured screams. Michael was in the *Cupola*, desperately trying to operate the SSRMS when the octopus turned its attention to him. Using its giant puss-yellow sucker, it tried to pull out one of the *Cupola* windows. As he screamed at the beast he woke up, his skin and hair damp.

What a weird dream – an octopus, tentacles and the *Cupola*? He needed to get to sleep. Tomorrow was going to be difficult enough. Deep breaths started to relax him as he tried to empty his whirring mind, but suddenly he realised. He had an idea what Jamie meant with his stuff about skateboard moves, videos and arms and he had to do something about it right now.

Inching back his curtain with the tips of his thumb and forefinger, Michael peered out. He could definitely hear Ralph's snoring. Everyone could hear Ralph's snoring, even above the constant hum, whine and bangs of the ISS. Buddy would have his headphones on and wouldn't hear anything. Steve was on a late timetable in the *Destiny* lab so that just left Sarah. All he had to do was get out without her hearing and he could get down to the *Cupola*.

Even though it was nearly eleven o'clock on Michael's GMT watch, it was daylight outside when he reached the *Cupola*. Gazing down on the land swiping from left to right, he saw the coast of Scotland, followed shortly by mainland Europe. He could have watched for hours, but he might only have minutes before someone got up to use the toilet and noticed he was missing.

'Come on...come on...' Michael muttered as he searched for the robotic workstation log. This held a record of every use of the SSRMS. Within seconds his details came up. It didn't take long to scan through them. He and Buddy had logged in to practice using the SSRMS before Ralph and Marat's EVA and there were only two other entries. The first was during the EVA itself and the second was when Steve and Ralph checked that the SSRMS was working properly after the accident. It was all perfectly normal. Then he switched to look at the robotic workstation log in the *Destiny* module.

That can't be, he thought. Maybe he was still dreaming. The records showed that he'd also been logged in to the *Destiny* workstation at exactly the same time as he was in the *Cupola*. Not only was that a physical impossibility, but it also proved that someone had stolen his ID and was willing to let him take the blame for Ralph's accident.

So now he knew *how* it had been done, he just had to prove who had done it.

'Psst!' said a voice suddenly from behind Michael, making him hop backwards. 'What are you doing?'

Michael scowled and pointed at the workstation logs.

Buddy shrugged. 'Not sure it proves anything…and anyway why are you out here? You know what Ralph said.'

'Couldn't sleep and I'm not letting her get away with it,' whispered Michael. 'Look again.'

Buddy screwed up his dark eyes and peered at the page of data.

'So how could I be logged on to two different places at the same time?' asked Michael.

'OK, but you can't trace anything back to Jia Li.'

'Everyone else was accounted for, apart from her,' said Michael. That means it has to be her.'

'What you need, Mike is some real evidence…'

'Like…a…video recording or something,' said Michael, a tiny flicker of a smile pulling up the edge of his lip.

'Whatever you're thinking of, Mike, it'd better be quick and silent. Someone's bound to get up soon and then you'll be in a heap more trouble than you already are.'

Chapter Twenty

'There are cameras all over the ISS. All we've got to do is look through the footage on each one at the time of Ralph's injury and then in the gap between setting up the PM4 experiment and Sarah finding one of the test tubes missing.'

'But that could take ages, Mike and we've got to be up and doing the XO3 stuff in six hours,' said Buddy. 'We could do it tomorrow when we've got some spare time? I'll be with you, so Ralph won't care.

'No, I want to do it now,' said Michael. 'It's too important to leave until tomorrow. If you want to go to bed, then go, but I'm doing it.'

Buddy rolled his eyes, nudged Michael to one side and scrolled down the screen of onboard video files. He typed in the time range and tapped his fingers on the desk as the system searched for the footage.

'According to this, if we put it on at twice the speed it should only take an hour,' said Michael.

Buddy nodded and pressed the fast-forward key.

Just over an hour later Buddy closed the system down.

'I don't get it,' said Michael, rubbing his face. 'I was sure we'd find something to link Jia Li to Ralph's accident and the test tube.'

'Yeah, it's weird. I don't understand how there could be nothing...and that bit of footage of you making your way back to *Destiny* with Cyril stuffed under your t-shirt makes things worse. It's the only thing that looks suspicious.'

Michael didn't reply.

'Look, dude, I've got to get some sleep. Promise me you won't do anything stupid. I need you to keep me sane up here, remember.'

Michael nodded, and Buddy left.

By now daylight was turning to a twilight, which bathed everything in an orangey-pink glow. How could planet earth be so beautiful and the subject of song lyrics, poems and art, yet so full of evil and hate, thought Michael? The news seemed to be full of stories about power, violence and arms struggles.

That's the word Jamie had used in his email: *Arms – it's vital to use your arms. It's amazing how useful they can be if you have them in the right place to start with.*

He's not just telling me to check the robotic workstation log, thought Michael, instinctively wrapping his battered hands around the controls. He's telling me to *use* the SSRMS. 'Come on then,' he whispered, 'let's see how far we can get you.'

This was going to be a challenge. Although he'd practised a few times during his training, he'd never manoeuvred the SSRMS across the ISS on his own, let alone used one of its most complex features. It had been designed so that one end of it could attach to part of the ISS, whilst the other stretched out to grab another section. The first end was then released to stretch out and grab the next section. It was like a metal, monster inchworm.

As the SSRMS hummed into life, Michael prayed no one would hear it. He used one of the monitors to practice a couple of manoeuvres whilst flexing the giant hand-like end effector. Doing it himself was so slow but he'd probably got Buddy involved enough already. If he wanted to prove Jia Li had been up to her old tricks, he'd have to do it alone.

His hands winced as he pushed, pulled and squeezed the controls, but he kept going. The SSRMS made its way along the length of the ISS on its mobile base system and then end over end to the Chinese module, stopping when it reached the top of the canister shape.

Four cameras protruded from it: two on the 'elbow'

and two on the 'hand'. But all he needed was to capture something on just one of them to prove that Jia Li was up to no good. He might not get anything tonight as it was late but, if he could get the SSRMS over to the *Dàdǎn* now, he could nip into the *Cupola* with Buddy in the morning and take another look.

He edged the end of the SSRMS towards one of the porthole windows on the *Dàdǎn* module. He couldn't afford to be caught spying, particularly given the trouble he was already in, but he had to get close enough to see inside. He took a long, slow breath in, tried to calm the shaking in his hands, flexed his disgruntled fingers and moved closer to the screens.

The first porthole looked into the galley. After a slight adjustment from left to right with his handset, Michael could see it was empty. No midnight feasts or anyone snaffling cookies and hot chocolate here then.

The second porthole was into the node that contained the sleep stations. Again, the curtains were drawn and there wasn't even a flicker of movement.

The morning would definitely be a better time, thought Michael, moving the SSRMS to the last window.

He pulled his hand controller back slowly to lift the end of the SSRMS away from the window when he saw a blurred shape dart across one of the screens. He stopped and moved back to the window. Now the image was as clear as a high definition television screen. He could see Marat, which wasn't odd in itself. He slept in the Chinese module. What was strange was why he was in the lab this time of night. He was looking into the Microgravity Science Glovebox (MSG), probably examining the super-fast-growing Chinese plants.

But as he was looking, Marat was talking to someone.

'Come on…come on. Move just a bit to your left…

please?'

First, he saw a pair of dainty, pale hands. But these hands didn't match the bullying, dark character they belonged to. He only needed to see a swish of a black ponytail to know it was Jia Li.

When she eventually moved across into Michael's camera view, he should have been elated, but the sight of Marat and Jia Li fighting...over a test tube...made the undigested hot chocolate and cookies curdle in his stomach.

'What d'you mean "they were fighting over a test tube"?' mumbled a sleepy Buddy as Michael rattled off everything he'd seen with the SSRMS.

'I mean exactly that,' said Michael, talking like his annoying sister when she was excited about a piece of gossip at school or a new horse poster for her bedroom. 'Jia Li had a test tube in her hand and Marat was...well he was sort of trying to take it from her.'

'And?' said Buddy, rubbing his eyes and showing Michael the back of his throat as he yawned.

'And he couldn't. Jia Li shoved him out of the way and stormed off,' said Michael, like this was a description of some action movie and not happening right here, right now.

Buddy's eyebrows were up in their startled starting positions but rose higher as Michael continued.

'I thought I'd lost them both when they walked off, but I just managed to get the SSRMS over in time to see her stuff the test tube under a pile of clothes in the laundry room.'

'Now hang on, Mike. I know I've just woken up from the most awesome dream about taking Laura Wells on the coolest space date ever, but even I can work out that something's not right there. Marat found the missing test tube in your sleep station – sorry to remind you. We found it, so what do we care about another test tube?'

Michael paused. 'But what if the test tube they found in Cyril wasn't the missing one, Buddy? What if Jia Li still has the test tube with the PM4 in it?'

Chapter Twenty-One

The *Destiny* lab was buzzing. This was the day they'd been too nervous to talk about; the day they were going to add XO3 to the PM4 samples; the day they might create a vaccine against cancer.

Sarah's bouncing and singing were a bit much for Michael's tired head. She looked different, too. They didn't get to bring many clothes up to the ISS and most of the crew wore cargo trousers and t-shirts, but today Sarah had tied her hair up differently and was wearing a pink and blue spotty shirt.

'Morning, guys,' said Ralph, ushering everyone towards him with his bandaged hand. 'I hope you had a good night's sleep and are ready for today. We could be making history here in a few hours. Steve, you'll be recording as we go and Marat, you'll be writing up the report on our findings to take back home. I'm sure I don't need to remind you that no one must talk about what we're doing today to anyone and the video footage and report stay with me until we're home again. Understood?'

Everyone nodded.

'You've got your own checks, exercise and experiments going on today but as soon as you know anything, Sarah, just come and get us.'

'Sure,' said Sarah, looking like she was on the blocks before a race.

As soon as the group had disbursed, Michael approached Ralph. 'Could I have a quick word please?'

Ralph looked away. 'To be honest, Michael, I don't really want to have a conversation right now.'

'Yeah, but I need to talk…'

'There's been too much talking, Michael. Why don't

we just get on with what we're supposed to be doing and think about Liz Matheson.' Ralph turned and left before Michael had a chance to tell him what he'd been up to the night before.

'Hey, Mike,' said Buddy from behind him. 'Don't be too hard on yourself. Everyone's finding it difficult to get their heads around it all.'

'I don't care, Buddy. I've had enough!'

Carrying out his carbon dioxide removal and air contamination checks were a relief for Michael – a mechanical activity that required very little thinking and absolutely no talking to anyone else. Buddy had to be in the room with him, but that was OK. He knew better than to start another conversation.

It wasn't until after lunch that Michael and Buddy had the perfect excuse to go to the *Dàdǎn* module. They'd asked Ralph if they could go and look at the accelerated plant growth experiments and he'd agreed; only Michael had something different in mind.

'You go and find Ru or Shen and ask them to explain what's happening with the experiment and I'm going to go searching through their dirty washing,' said Michael, already on his way.

The laundry room wasn't just for dirty washing. It was stuffed full of all sorts of rubbish ready for them to jettison on their re-entry to earth. Michael knew exactly where to look. At least he thought he did. He pulled at the piles of folded washing, running his hand over every item and into each pocket. Nothing.

'Planning to do some laundry tonight are we, Michael May?'

Michael spun around as fast as microgravity would allow and glared at the owner of the barbed voice.

'Now, why would you be searching through dirty

washing?' asked Jia Li, arms folded and eyes glaring.

Michael backed away, bumping into the doorway. 'Er...I put some of my cargo trousers in here and must have left my headphones in one of the pockets.'

Jia Li look around, before whispering, 'I do not think you are going to find what you are looking for in there, Michael. But if you are patient and do not meddle in things that you do not understand, you will find what you are looking for soon. Believe me.'

What was she on about now, thought Michael, as he finished patting down a pair of trousers? She was making less sense than usual. And why would he believe her after everything she'd done?

Buddy was peering through the MSG at green shoots that were at least one centimetre tall when Michael arrived. 'Look at these, dude,' he said, not registering the dejected look on Michael's face. 'Aren't they just awesome? They've grown this tall in four days. Just imagine what that means for growing food in space in the future.'

The boys stayed for what they thought was a polite length of time, asking Ru and Shen all the right sorts of questions, before returning to the *Destiny* module to do their exercise.

'Go on then, Mike. You've obviously got something going on in your head. What is it?' asked Buddy, strapping on what looked like oversized braces and setting the treadmill speed.

Michael shrugged. Even his best friend seemed to find it hard to believe what was going on. Perhaps he ought to keep it to himself?

By the time his exercise was over, Michael had time for a quick wash before they were due to meet Sarah. Staring in the mirror at the unhappy face in front of him, Michael knew he had to think of something else. He had to think of a way of proving Jia Li's guilt.

The atmosphere in the *Destiny* lab was like an operating theatre; The surgeons gathered to perform a brand new procedure that was extremely risky, yet could lead to a significant medical breakthrough. After the business with the test tube, Ralph had already told Michael that he'd just be observing. He stood silently as Buddy and Sarah slipped on their protective clothing.

Steve held a video camera from one side and Marat had his laptop ready to write up the experiment notes.

'Are you ready, Buddy?' asked Sarah.

Buddy swallowed, then nodded.

This was such a big deal; only a handful of people in the entire universe knew what they were about to do and even fewer knew what it could mean for Jamie's mum.

Ralph and Sarah had weighed the contents of the first sack of XO3 and decanted it into smaller screw-top containers. There was only one sugar-cube sized piece of the pinkish crystal in each one.

'OK, so the first step is to test the PM4 and take the PH level. We know it can alter in microgravity, but we need to know by how much,' said Sarah. 'Then we add the XO3 in increasing amounts from left to right as labelled.'

Michael looked at the test tube rack in the MSG. There were now four rows of five plus the test tube found in Cyril.

With the humming of the ISS the only sound, Buddy released a small plastic wallet from the Velcro on the side of the MSG and removed a tube of thin cardboard strips from it. He closed the wallet, secured it to the Velcro, and with trembling hands, pushed a cardboard strip down through a thin slot and into the first test tube. He repeated the exercise twenty-one times before removing them one by one.

'Test tube one is six,' said Buddy, reading from the scale on the strip. 'Test tube two is six also.'

Steve kept the video trained on Buddy and Sarah whilst Marat tapped each result into his spreadsheet.

'Test tube twenty is six,' repeated Buddy, in a mechanical voice.

'Let me guess,' said Steve, raising his eyebrows. 'Test tube twenty-one is six. I think we get this now. The preservative has had the same effect in each test tube. The PH levels are identical. Now we add the XO3. Can we move on now? My arm's starting to ache.'

'Test tube twenty-one is...wait a minute,' said Buddy, screwing up his eyes and looking again. He glanced up at Michael for a split-second. 'Test tube twenty-one is seven.'

'What?' said Sarah, looking at Buddy to see if he was joking.

Buddy held the strip out, so she could see for herself. The reading was definitely seven.

'How can that be?' said Steve, the camera now wobbling on his shoulder. 'How can one test tube...'

Ralph covered his face with the palms of his hands and blew out a long breath. 'It's obvious, isn't it,' he said, looking straight at Michael. 'It's not one of the originals.'

'What do you mean?' said Marat.

'As I just said, it can't be one of the originals, Marat. Twenty have the same reading but the last one, the one we found in Michael's sleep station, is different.'

'I don't get it,' said Sarah.

'It's really simple, Sarah,' said Ralph, putting his hand on Michael's shoulder. 'We should have believed him. The test tube we found in Michael's sleep station can't be the missing one. It was planted there by the person who really took it.'

'That is ridiculous,' said Marat. 'If he was hiding a test tube in his sleep station, it must be the missing one.'

'Let me show you. Sarah, could you please test the liquid...I've got a feeling that there's nothing deadly in it at all,' said Ralph.

The room was now like an exam room; jangling with nerves and expectation. The only noise was Marat, tapping at his laptop.

'You're absolutely right, Ralph,' croaked Sarah. 'It's probably just water.'

As relief flowed through Michael's body, red coloured his face. There were now five pairs of eyes staring at him.

'I'm sorry, Michael,' said Ralph.

'Me too,' added Sarah, pulling her hands out of the MSG and patting Michael's forearm.

'I'm sure Michael's grateful for your apologies etcetera, but that kinda leaves us in a bit of an awkward situation, doesn't it?' said Buddy

'I am not sure, "awkward" is the word,' said Ralph. 'It means that Michael had nothing to do with the missing test tube and that it must be someone else.'

'It's not one of us,' said Michael under his breath.

'What did you say?' asked Sarah.

'It's not one of us,' repeated Michael, looking at everyone in turn. 'It's...Er...Jia Li...I mean Yue...I knew as soon as I saw her, but no one believed me. This means she's still got the PM4 sample somewhere on the ISS and we need to get it back.'

'I don't think it's wise for us all to go looking for Yue,' said Marat.

Typical Marat. He'd made absolutely no contribution and now, suddenly, he was telling them what to do.

'I disagree,' said Michael, looking Marat as straight in the face as he dared. 'I think we should all go and find her right now. Who knows what she's doing with that sample. You're both wearing protective clothing and she's swanning around with it in a test tube. And, just to let you know, she's not called Yue...her real name is Jia Li!'

Steve shattered the uncomfortable silence with a single clap of his hands. 'I agree with Michael. He's one hundred per cent certain that Yue or Jia Li has something to do with all this. He told me why Bob Sturton had to throw her off the Children's Moon Program and you don't change your name unless you've got something to hide. We've got to get on to this straight away before something worse happens.'

Sarah and Buddy made sure that the samples were resealed and that everything, including the XO3 bags, was safely locked in the MSG.

'We'll carry on when we've sorted this out,' said Ralph, making the first move towards the *Harmony* node and straight through to the *Dàdǎn* module.

They swam like a shoal of giant fish towards their target.

'Well, where is she, Ru?' Ralph was asking by the time Michael arrived.

'If you mean Yue, she is having her leisure break,' said Ru, still smiling despite the downturned fish faces around him. 'Can I help you with something, my *Fortis* friends?'

'We need to talk to her, now, Ru. It's really important,' said Ralph, already turning to head towards the sleep stations. 'Sorry, I can't stop.'

They squeezed into the tiny area by the sleep stations. 'Yue, are you there? We need to talk to you?' called Ralph.

There was no answer.

Steve didn't hesitate. He bounded forward and pulled back the curtain. 'Empty.'

'Now what?' said Buddy. 'We know she's not in the *Destiny* or *Dàdǎn* modules but she could be anywhere else...in the Russian or Japanese segment or any of the nodes.

'We split up and search,' said Michael. 'Marat and I will go to *Inceptor 1*, Sarah and Buddy go to the *Kibo* and *Zvezda* modules and Ralph and Steve search the *Cupola*, nodes, airlocks and toilets. Meet back in the *Destiny* lab in twenty minutes.'

Buddy gave Michael an, 'are you sure you know what you're doing?' look, but everyone else nodded and disappeared.

'I am surprised you want to go searching with me,' said Marat, as Michael set off towards the docked *Inceptor 1*. 'I have a strong feeling that you do not like me much.'

What could he say? If he was honest, he'd have to agree with Marat, but there wasn't time for any of this. Michael didn't reply, and Marat followed him silently to *Inceptor 1*'s docking port.

'Hey, look,' said Michael, using the cables on the side of the wall to pull himself forward as fast as he could go. 'The hatch is open. You know who's got to be in there, don't you and we're just about to catch her red-handed!'

Chapter Twenty-Two

Marat glided up to the open, metal door and peered inside.

'She's got to be in there,' said Michael. 'There's no other reason the hatch would be open.'

'I'll go in,' said Marat. 'I speak Chinese.'

'No!' said Michael, shoving Marat aside. 'I've let everyone else take charge up to now. I'm going in and you can wait for me here.'

Apart from a few bags of equipment, *Inceptor 1* was empty. There was no sign of Jia Li. It didn't make sense.

Michael turned and pulled himself through to the service module. If someone curled up in here and piled some of the supplies on top of them, they could just about hide. But after moving oxygen tanks, water bottles and the parachute bags for landing, he was left looking at the bare floor.

He was about to return to Marat when he heard a thud; like a heavy footstep on a wooden floor. Then another. He pulled himself to the outside wall and put his ear to the metal. There was now a scratching sound; like the mice behind the skirting boards in his granny's house. Something or someone was there.

He bent forwards, yanked up the hatch and dived into *Vader's* cramped capsule, straight on top of Jia Li.

'Michael May, what are you doing here?' she hissed, pushing him into the side of the capsule with the back of her forearm.

'Hey! Get off. What am I doing in here? I'm looking for you. The question is, what are you doing here and what's in those?' he said, pointing to three lunchbox-sized metal containers behind her.

'It is nothing to do with you,' said Jia Li, stuffing the

containers into a sack. 'Why don't you go away and let me get on with what I'm doing? You have no idea who or what you are dealing with, Michael May.'

'Well, seeing as you're in someone else's vehicle, I reckon you're taking something that doesn't belong to you…and not for the first time. Why don't you show me what's in that sack if you've nothing to hide?' He made a grab for the sack but as he pushed himself forwards, Jia Li squeezed between him and the outside of the lunar lander and out of the hatch. Michael twisted and spun after her like a bullet. She was just ahead of him, but far enough… 'Argh!' Something smashed against his temple. He put his hand to his head and looked at the dark red smudge that had appeared on his palm. By the time his blurred vision got him to the hatch, it was too late. The light rapidly reduced to a tiny sliver before disappearing.

Michael's stomach fell just like it had on his first zero-gravity dive in the *Vomit Comet* as the hatch handle moved to *Locked* right in front of him. She'd shut him in. That demented, evil, warped girl had locked him in *Inceptor 1*.

He forced his bruised hands to the hatch lever and tried to move it in the opposite direction. Sometimes these doors were stiff but this one wasn't moving at all. He could just about make out voices beyond the hatch. That would be Marat catching her in the act. For once he was glad he had Marat on his side and couldn't care less how rude he was to Jia Li. She deserved everything she got. The raised voices continued and although Michael hadn't a clue what the Chinese words meant, he recognised an argument.

Michael banged his fist on the hatch, just to remind Marat where he was, but the voices suddenly trailed off into the distance, leaving a dark, lonely silence. Perhaps Marat was taking Jia Li to Ru and Shen, or to find the *Fortis* crew. But why hadn't he opened the hatch first?

Twenty minutes later and still slumped against the hatch door, Michael's thoughts drifted towards a new, horrific possibility; that he'd been shut in on purpose and that the only people who knew had disappeared.

He tried not to press the light button on his watch. Its pathetic beam wouldn't help him see much and, knowing how long he'd been trapped, wasn't going to help him get out. There was water on board, but without power to *Inceptor 1*, there were no lights and, more importantly, no ventilation system. At some point, he'd run out of oxygen. A stabbing pain now pulsed in his temple. The others were bound to find him soon and once they saw his head, they'd have to believe him about Jia Li.

Michael jolted. He must have dozed off, but how long for? The heat reminded him of hiding under his bed covers as a child, trying to get in an extra bit of reading late into the night without his parents knowing. Eventually, he'd get so hot and stuffy that he'd have to come up for air. But this wasn't some childish rebellion – this was getting serious now.

He slammed his fist against the side of *Inceptor 1* again...and again. It made an echoless thud. He needed something heavier. Using the tiny glow-worm green light from his watch, he scanned the capsule. Most objects were attached to the walls or instrument panels. The only thing he could remove was one of the metal buckles from a seat. This made a satisfying metallic clank on the hatch. A few of these and surely everyone would hear him.

'How long do you think he's been in here?'

'I don't know, Buddy,' said Sarah, clamping her hand to her mouth. 'I last saw him a couple of hours ago when we all went off to look for Yue. Oh my god, look! There's blood on his head! What are we going to tell his parents?'

said Sarah, oversized water globules covering her eyes like unflattering goggles.

'Hang on a minute. I think I can feel a pulse. Here, you have a feel,' said Buddy, wiping his eyes on his sleeve and making room for Sarah.

Michael resembled a floating mummy as Sarah lifted his wrist. Her eyes darted as she concentrated on what the forefinger and middle finger of her right hand could detect.

'He's alive, Buddy. I can definitely feel a weak pulse.'

'Mike...Mike,' said Buddy, gently patting him on the cheek. 'Come on, dude. That's enough of putting the frighteners on me. I've got this really awesome joke to tell you, but you've got to wake up first.'

Slowly, Michael's eyelids slid upwards, like an old, juddering, electric garage door. 'Er...not...not sure I'm... quite in the mood for one of your jokes.'

'Don't worry, Michael. Just stay where you are for the moment until you feel OK again. What were you doing in *Inceptor 1?*' Sarah asked, dabbing at the oozing wound on his head.

'Marat and I went to look for Jia Li,' he said, trying to right himself from a lying position.

'Yes, he came to find us about twenty minutes ago. He said you'd had an argument and stormed off. He tried to find you but couldn't.'

'Yeah, we looked everywhere, Mike. Didn't think you'd have gone to look in *Inceptor 1,*' said Buddy. 'That was a bit far out, wasn't it?'

'But I went there with Marat,' said Michael, now doubting whether he was really awake or in some parallel dream. 'We both went to *Inceptor 1* to look for...'

'Dude, Marat was with us when we found you. You obviously banged your head in there and knocked yourself out for a bit. We found you just in the entrance to the hatch.'

'But I was locked in,' said Michael, someone crashing symbols inside his head.

'No, Mike. I think you're a bit confused. The hatch door was open when we found you.'

None of this made sense. Buddy and Sarah seemed to be talking a different language. What they were saying was the complete opposite of the truth. He'd been right about Jia Li all along and now his worst nightmare was coming true. Somehow Marat was involved too.

'Listen, Mike. Let's get you back to the *Destiny* lab where Sarah can have a proper look at you and dress that cut. Then we can talk,' said Buddy, already guiding Michael out of the docking area and down into the *Harmony* node.

There was no point telling them what'd happened. Right now, he didn't have the energy and anyway, it sounded like Jia Li and Marat had covered their tracks. They wouldn't believe him.

The rest of the *Fortis* crew were back in the *Destiny* lab as Michael arrived.

'Oh, crikey. What happened to you, Michael?' said Steve, bounding over to him.

'Er...I sort of got locked in *Inceptor 1* and banged my head,' he said, deciding that the truth would be far less believable than what he'd just said.

Sarah looped a really unattractive bandage around his head and almost over one eye, whilst Buddy made lame pirate jokes and Ralph filled out an accident report. It read 'hit head inside *Inceptor 1*'. It had to say that because of the stupid experiment they were doing. Otherwise, he'd have written 'was savagely attacked by a thief, liar, con-artist and cheat, who is trying to steal top-secret, life-changing medical research for her own warped purposes.'

Once everyone had stopped fussing over him and the

painkillers had chased the fog from his brain, Michael
asked if the others had uncovered anything during their
search for Jia Li.

'We looked for over an hour and couldn't find her,' said
Ralph, 'but then she turned up here. She said she'd heard
we were looking for her and what could she do to help.'

'And?'

'I came straight out with it and asked her if she knew
anything about a missing experiment sample or my
accident,' said Ralph.

Michael waited.

'Her answer was odd…in fact everything about her was
odd. She looked and sounded totally deflated. She said
something about coming to see that you were OK later and
to pass on a message to you.'

'About what?' asked Michael. Knowing Jia Li, her
message was bound to be some sort of veiled threat.

'She wanted to say sorry for the cupboard and that she's
going to make things right, whatever that means.'

None of this made sense. How could she be apologising
for locking him in a cupboard on the CMP, when she'd just
assaulted him and locked him in *Inceptor 1*?

'I'm not sure what else we can do,' said Sarah. 'We've
looked everywhere, spoken to everyone and right now,
our experiment is probably more important than ever. We
owe it to Jamie's mum to keep going and the rest of the
stuff will just have to wait.'

'I agree,' said Steve. 'We've got to get on with our
mission. All this suspicion and mistrust is going to affect
our work.'

'Why don't you go and get some rest before dinner and
we'll talk more then,' said Ralph. 'Sarah and Buddy will
finish their experiment this evening, so at least we'll find
out if we've got something positive to talk about.'

Michael didn't need to be persuaded. He'd tell Ralph later about what he'd seen with the SSRMS cameras and show him Jamie's encrypted email too, but for now, he was done. He pulled down the bandage, already slowly creeping up his forehead, and made off to his sleep station. Although only inches from chaos, the drawn curtain felt like a symbolic cutting off from the world and Michael was alone at last.

He clamped his eyes shut and tried to rid his head of the tangled ball of thought threads, but it was useless. There was no way he'd sleep. Flipping open his laptop, he checked his private email inbox. There was one from Charlotte, which instantly cheered him up. She told him about Adam Painter being selected for the schools' county football team and attached a copy of the *Andoverford News*. There was a picture of Michael on the surface of the moon with the caption 'May's Mission to Moon,' and an article full of the usual assortment of people claiming to know him, or to have seen him once at a supermarket or crossing the road in Andoverford.

He clicked on the next email. It was from Jamie. He hadn't had a second to let him know what had happened and wasn't sure if he could find a clever way of hiding the information anyway. But that didn't matter when he read Jamie's message: *Got all the information you will ever need. Don't worry, Mike. It'll all be good. Stay safe and don't be too hard on JL. Thanks for what you're doing. JM*

Michael shook his head. If only Jamie knew how difficult it'd been staying safe in this place. But what did he mean by 'it'll all be good' and 'don't be too hard on JL'?

Chapter Twenty-Three

A couple of rounds of *First Sniper Force*, imagining his target was Jia Li and Michael felt calm enough to go and join the others for dinner. He wasn't particularly hungry and couldn't get what Jamie had written out of his head.

As he inched his way through what was a minuscule dinner for him, his stomach rebelled, making him wretch.

'I think everyone would understand if you wanted to head back to your sleep station, dude,' said Buddy under his breath. 'You can even take some of my salt and vinegar crisps for later if you like?'

Michael smiled. He must look bad if Buddy was offering him some of his crisp rations.

'We've got a quick call with Mission Control, guys, before we get on with our experiment,' said Ralph, as the rest of the crew were clearing away their rubbish. 'They want a status update. It shouldn't take long.'

That's all he needed, thought Michael; having to smile and be positive when he felt the exact opposite. And what was the Mission Control team going to think when they saw two of them in bandages now?

Back in the *Destiny* lab, the crew found their most comfortable positions. Some hovered where they were, folding their arms to keep themselves from floating into odd positions; others, like Buddy, didn't care and couldn't quite manage to stay in one spot. He drifted one way for a while, before correcting himself and then going back the other way.

Michael pulled himself to the side of the module and slipped his foot under one of the floor straps.

'It'll be about forty seconds until we're in satellite range,' said Ralph, checking his watch.

The screen flickered with streaks of colour, but no sound, before it sprang into life with a full-sized picture of John Dell's smiling face.

'Good evening to the *Fortis* crew on the ISS. It's Saturday the 16th August and this is John Dell calling from Mission Control for a mission update.'

The crew smiled and lifted a hand to the screen. This wouldn't be broadcast, but Bob Sturton had always told them to show how much they appreciated this amazing experience.

'How's that hand of yours doing, Ralph?' asked John.

'Oh, I'll live, thanks,' replied Ralph, holding a less thickly bandaged hand up to show him. 'Michael decided to join me earlier though when he lost a fight with a metal hatch.'

The familiar itching trickled over Michael's cheeks, soon accompanied by a fast travelling spread of colour. 'I'll live too,' he mumbled. 'It's nothing.'

'So apart from two injuries, what's your status report please?' asked John.

But before Ralph could tell John the pre-approved story about stem cells and allergy experiments and the stuff about testing the effects of space on growing bodies, the screen flickered, and they were suddenly looking at a still picture of the *Harmony* node 2. The date was the 12th of August, the time, 12.06 and at the bottom of the screen, there was a play button.

'What? That's when Marat and I were out doing our EVA,' said Ralph, turning to look at his blank-faced partner.

'This is Jamie Matheson, Mission Control Flight Activities Officer,' said a voice over the picture.

Michael and Buddy exchanged glances.

'I know that interfering with Mission Control protocol will probably mean the end of my short career in the space industry, but I just can't leave my two best buddies and some new ones up in the ISS in such danger.'

The play button was activated, and the still screen became video footage. Within seconds, a clear image of Jia Li flashed into view.

'I knew it,' said Michael, moving closer to the screen.

Looking around, she pulled herself to the power circuit that had been turned off to allow Ralph and Marat to conduct their repairs, and with a quick flick, switched it back on.

Sarah let out a small whimpering noise, Marat shook his head and Ralph stared.

Then the video froze before jumping forward sixty seconds when Jia Li appeared at the robotic workstation in the *Destiny* lab. She pulled out a piece of paper and tapped something into the laptop, before disappearing.

'That's the ID she stole from me,' said Michael. 'That's why the log shows that I was on both robotic workstations at the same time.'

'I don't understand,' said Steve, pulling at his chin. 'We looked through all of the footage…'

He didn't have time to finish before the next piece of the video began. It was in the *Destiny* lab at 18.00.

'Let me guess what we're going to see now,' said Ralph, looking over at a disbelieving Michael.

'We were all at dinner then,' said Steve. 'Oh yeah, all except one person, who was in her sleep station feeling sick.'

Sarah's face had gone the same shade as one of Michael's best blushes and she looked ready to explode as she watched Jia Li take one of the PM4 test tubes before adding a few drops of something from a bottle she was holding to the remaining ones. 'She doesn't even look nervous or worried that she's tampering with something that's potentially lethal!' said Sarah. 'Where did she get the information about the PM4 anyway? I thought you said that only three other people knew about it, Ralph?'

Ralph shrugged.

The screenshot changed again. It was Jamie.

'I'm sorry, John and to everyone else at Mission Control. I just need a few minutes with the *Fortis* crew and you can have them back,' said an anxious-looking Jamie. 'I can't receive you, so you'll just have to listen. I probably don't have long until I'm taken off the air.'

From the background, Michael could tell he was somewhere else than Mission Control.

'He's taken over their communication system,' Buddy mouthed to Michael.

'You're probably wondering how these sections of video are missing from the footage you looked at. Well if you look at them very carefully, there is a glitch every now and again. That's where someone's cut a piece of video out of the ISS recording. It's a good idea, but quite an amateurish job. Whoever did it either forgot or didn't know that all footage is streamed back to Mission Control and recorded. It didn't take me long to cross match the two and find the missing pieces.'

Even though they'd now got actual proof that Jia Li was guilty, to see it all captured on video shocked Michael.

'I wonder if he's got footage of her going into your sleep station and taking Cyril, Mike?' asked Buddy. 'And there must be a section of her arguing with Marat over the test tube?'

Ralph looked at Michael for an explanation.

Michael would explain, but there was clearly something else from the look on Jamie's face.

'I know you're trying to get your head around all this, guys, but I have to tell you something else. It was Jia Li who sent me a message to look through the video footage. I've no idea why, because she's just ended up incriminating herself, but there has to be something else going on.'

A pinball of panic bounced around Michael's stomach. He swung around to look at Marat. He'd gone.

'Not sure what good it's going to do either of them,' said Buddy. 'It's not like they can get away from here, is it? What are they going to do, get in one of the spacecraft and head home?'

'They wouldn't?' said Sarah, looking at Ralph for an answer.

'What?' said Michael, holding his palms up in mock surprise. 'You don't think that, having stolen a PM4 sample, injuring Ralph, incriminating me and goodness knows what else they've done, that they'd think twice about trying to leave, do you?'

'But they'd be leaving seven of us up here with only six seats back to earth?' said Sarah.

'Exactly!' said Michael. 'They don't care.'

'But they'd only have one sample of PM4. Without the XO3, I don't really see what they'd gain from taking it,' said Sarah.

Michael's brain suddenly served up an image he'd already dismissed. It was one of those 'lightning bolt' moments people talked about. 'I know,' he shouted, pushing himself off towards the *Harmony* node 2 and on to the *Dàdǎn* module. 'I've worked out what's happening. We've got to get to Marat and Jia Li before it's too late.'

Ralph thanked a bemused-looking John before following Michael. It was the same clumsy shoal of human fish that had set out before to look for Jia Li, but this time Michael knew what was going on and what he'd find.

'Have you seen Jia Li...I mean Yue?' asked Ralph as they piled into the *Dàdǎn* module.

Ru and Shen lurched backwards from their laptops when they saw the five-strong *Fortis* crew. 'My friends, you all look so unhappy. Is there a problem we can help you with, please?' said Ru.

'Er...yeah...I mean, we need to find Yue,' said Michael, forcing himself to say the strange, lying name. 'Do you know where she is?'

'Yes, she is very popular today. Marat has just been here, and we sent him to the IDA-3, where Yue is testing the airlock and hatch of our new port. We finished building it yesterday and with the help of Marat, have moved our spacecraft, Áng, to its new home. It is very exciting for us. It means that we can travel to and from our own port without the need to rely on our very kind friends.'

'You know what that also means don't you?' said Michael already setting off towards the new International Docking Adaptor (IDA).

'It means you could be right, Mike. They could be idiotic enough to be thinking about taking Áng and trying to get home.'

A minute later, the five solemn astronauts reached the new docking adaptor.

'I'm not sure you want to be doing that,' said Ralph, making the two fugitives jump.

Jia Li spun around.

Michael waited for the barrage of caustic words to tumble out of her mouth but there were none. She simply shrugged, smiled and offered the sack she was holding.

'What are you doing?' Marat pushed forwards and grabbed the back of Jia Li's shirt. 'That belongs to me.'

The sleek, dark hair that Michael had come to loathe swished from side to side. 'No, Marat. That is not true.'

'We had a deal. We can still do it. We have what we need, and we can get back on our own,' said Marat.

Ralph moved forwards, almost like he had to rather than wanted to. 'So, go on, Marat. What exactly are you up to?'

Marat gave one of his steely, emotionless looks, still holding on to Jia Li's shirt.

'I can tell you what they're up to,' said Michael suddenly from behind. He wasn't having this. He wasn't giving Jia Li or Marat time to squirm their way out of this. 'I don't know how, but they must have found out about our PM4 experiment. They made sure that Jia Li was on the Chinese mission so that she could steal one of our samples and probably sell it for a huge amount of money. We know you fixed the video recordings – we've seen the backups that go to Mission Control. That's how we know you took the test tube, Jia Li.'

Marat's face remained stony.

'So why would you want the test tube then?' said Michael, the words cascading out of his mouth like a waterfall. 'Well, that wouldn't make any sense if that's all you had, would it. But you've got that sack, haven't you?'

Ralph held out his hand. 'I'd like to look inside the sack please, Yue, I mean Jia Li. If you haven't got anything to hide you won't mind, will you?'

'They've got containers of XO3 in there,' said Michael.

'What?' said Sarah. 'That's impossible.'

'No, it's not. We didn't just bring back our sixteen kilos of XO3 from the moon, did we, Marat?'

Marat gave a thin, smug smile and shook his head.

'If you look in that sack, you'll see extra XO3 samples,' said Michael.

'Hang on a minute, though,' said Sarah, scratching her head. 'How could Marat get hold of XO3 samples when he was in *Vader* the whole time?'

'Don't you tell me you left *Vader* unmanned and went

off on your own, Marat,' said Ralph, moving towards him. 'Of all the stupid, selfish, dangerous and idiotic things to do!'

'OK, Ralph,' said Steve, holding a palm up to each man. 'Can we just calm it down a little, please? We're in a really confined space and I don't want things getting out of control.'

'You left *Vader* to get your own samples of XO3, didn't you?' said Michael. 'That's why the spare spacesuit was dirty, wasn't it?'

'Yes,' replied Marat, so quietly that it was just audible.

'So that's why you weren't there when we got back... it was nothing to do with looking for us somewhere else,' said Buddy, pushing past Sarah to get near Marat. 'Do you know I could have died out there while you were swanning around helping yourself?'

'I think you are overreacting,' said Marat.

'He tampered with your EMU,' said Jia Li, suddenly.

'Hold your mouth!' Marat yanked the neck of her shirt. 'Remember what I told you.'

'What does she mean, Marat?' asked Michael, moving closer.

Jia Li looked at Marat and hesitated...'If Ralph was unable to make the moon mission, there would be a better chance of no one noticing the oxygen and CO2 readouts. With so much going on, two teenagers wouldn't think about checking the systems again. With less oxygen, it would take you and Buddy longer to collect your samples...'

'...Giving Marat time to collect his own,' finished Ralph.

'I just needed an hour,' said Marat, as if he was talking about getting his weekly groceries. 'I did not intend to let so much oxygen out of your tank.'

'Can you hear yourselves?' shouted Sarah. 'This has turned from some kind of Cold War-type drug spying into something far more sinister. Trying to harm a child, Marat. What kind of monster are you? I'm not listening to any more of this.'

Michael noticed Ralph fiddling with the end of his bandage. 'So, my mission to the moon gets cut because you two are greedy, heartless robots without a caring bone in your bodies. You've left me with a hand that doesn't function properly, work that I can't do and all because you thought you were more important than me. We've known each other for years, Marat. How could you?'

Marat rolled his eyes as if he was bored and for a second, Michael thought that Ralph might take a swipe at him with his good hand.

'Just give me the sack, Jia Li. Sarah, I want you to lock it in the MSG please,' said Ralph, calmer again.

'Oh, and we're going to need that test tube as well before we can go,' said Buddy.

'What test tube?' Marat pretended to pat down his pockets. I do not have a test tube.'

Ralph nodded to Michael.

Michael held out his hand and waited.

Marat gave him a 'you win some, you lose some' look before he reached down to a long pocket in his green cargo trousers, pulled the Velcro flap up and lifted out the test tube.

'I knew you'd do the right thing in the end,' said Ralph.

But before Michael could take the test tube, Marat jumped backwards, pulling Jia Li towards him and tightening his arm around her neck.

'Do not come any closer or I will open it,' he said. 'And do not try anything stupid. I have spent my whole life dealing with stupid people.'

'Hey now, Marat,' said Ralph, flashing a look of panic. 'We don't want you doing anything you'll regret.'

'The only thing I regret is trusting Jia Li to perform some simple tasks,' bellowed Marat. Having been quiet for most of the week he suddenly burst into life. He clenched his teeth, flexed the sides of his jaw and started to take large, loud breaths in and out. 'I am the one who got into the NASA laboratory and discovered the real plans for this mission and I am the one who made sure that Zian Peng was off the mission. All you had to do was what I told you!' he shouted, squeezing his arm tighter around Jia Li's neck.

'I did, I did,' said Jia Li. 'I got the sample for you and I did the other things you asked me to.'

'With your history, I thought you would be a good asset, but you failed. Now you have to pay the price of failure.' Marat unscrewed the lid of the test tube and brought it up to Jia Li's face.

Chapter Twenty-Four

'OK, Marat. There's no need to do anything silly,' said Michael, trying to steady the racing in his chest. 'You do know what you're holding, don't you?'

'Yes, he's right,' agreed Ralph, nodding frantically. 'If you want to talk about this, we've got as long as you like.'

Marat shook his head. 'I decide what happens next.'

'What do you want?' asked Michael, without thinking.

'I don't think you are in a position to ask me anything, Michael,' said Marat, tightening the test tube lid. 'I am in control now and I am going to tell *you* what to do. I want everyone to leave, but you.'

'Look, Marat, if you think I'm going to leave Michael on his own with...'

'Ralph, you do not have a choice. Leave or you will force me to do something unpleasant,' said Marat, jerking his forearm against Jia Li's throat.

Michael noticed the fear in Jia Li's face, something he'd not seen before and a tiny part of him felt sorry for her. He nodded to Ralph.

Marat waited. 'Good. Now Jia Li is going to drink this sample,' he said, holding up the test tube that had caused so much trouble on the ISS.

'Er...hang on a minute. You don't want to do that. You know what's in it. That's mad. Why don't you just give it to me, Marat?'

'You don't listen very well, Michael,' said Marat. 'This substance is only dangerous if it gets into the bloodstream and I do not intend that to happen.'

'But if Jia Li drinks it, it will eventually get into her bloodstream and then she'll most likely develop...'

'Cancer!' shouted Marat at full volume. 'Yes, let's say the

word that people are afraid to say. Cancer. It kills millions of people every year. In fact, it killed almost three million people in China alone last year,' he said, looking at Jia Li.

'OK, but what's the point of making Jia Li drink the sample?' said Michael, trying to second-guess Marat's runaway train of thought.

'...Because you are going to go and get me a sample of XO3.'

'What are you on about?'

'We know from the information that I obtained...'

'You mean stole.'

'If you prefer the word stole, then I can use it for you... the information that I stole told us that NASA scientists believed from a previous probe sample, that there was a substance on the far side of the moon, which could be used to obliterate the effects of the PM4 protein and therefore the development of cancer in humans.'

'Yes, I know all that, but it's been locked away and there's no way you're getting hold of it,' said Michael as forcefully as he dared.

'Unless *she* drinks this,' said Marat, holding up the test tube. 'Then you will have to give me some of the samples you collected, as an antidote. You know that without it she might die, and I know that none of you people will let that happen. She carries the antidote in her bloodstream and my team at home will be able to replicate it and create a synthetic version to get out into the market.'

Michael couldn't quite believe what Marat was saying. He was talking about putting substances not yet tested on the human body inside Jia Li and using her as a carrier.

He had to think ultra-fast now. There was no way he was going to get the XO3 samples for him, but how was he going to stop Marat from making Jia Li drink the contents of the test tube? For all he knew, she might die immediately and despite everything, he couldn't let that happen.

'Er…before I get it for you…' said Michael, trying to stop his voice from wavering, 'just tell me how you managed to get Jia Li on a space mission after what happened at the CMP?'

Jia Li glanced at Marat, who nodded and relaxed his grip on her.

With a hesitant and wary voice that Michael didn't recognise, Jia Li began to talk. 'I was the best in my year at high school and achieved the highest science grades ever recorded in my exams. My friends…yes, I did have some friends…they and my family thought I would go into medicine and become a doctor or surgeon.'

Michael tried not to show his horror at the thought of Jia Li being responsible for other people's health or well-being. 'So, what happened?'

'What happened is what often happens in communist states when someone is talented.'

Michael shrugged.

'Usually, the state takes that person and makes them even better at their talent. You will have seen it with gymnasts and athletes. You cannot refuse this offer of help and in return, you and your family are treated with respect and honour as you pursue your activity.'

'So, the state made you into an astronaut, then?' said Michael.

Jia Li paused. 'Not exactly. With me, it was a little different. I was spotted by the state and given the opportunity to study space science. As you will know in your training, Michael, China has wanted to be part of space exploration for many years but been refused by uncooperative, small-minded countries, like the USA. A few weeks after I started studying on the Shenzhou programme, a pharmaceutical company approached me.

They offered my family additional funding if I helped them with their research. It was so much more money than I was offered by our state and they promised free medical care also.'

Michael's face must have shown his surprise.

'Yes, I know this seems strange to you western people, but in my country, these sorts of things just do not happen. I was being taken through my astronaut training by the state, whilst being offered a deal by a company who would take care of my sick grandparents and family. It was an opportunity I could not reject. I would still get my training and possibly a chance to become an astronaut and my family would be safe, secure and comfortable for life.'

After two years of hating Jia Li and what she did on the CMP; after two years of wondering whether he would have been here had it not been for her undoubted sabotage on the CMP; after all the problems she'd caused and the bad feelings she'd created...he pitied her. She was like the bully at school without her band of supporters, without her cheerleaders, without the people around her to egg her on.

'So, who is the company?' asked Michael, wondering if this was going too far. 'Was that their picture on your bookmark? Was that who you were talking to the other night?'

Jia Li smiled – this time looking almost genuine. 'You do not need to know their name,' she said, 'but you can know that they are a large company who have great influence on the medical world. The words on the bookmark translate as "progress is not an option".'

'And they asked you to cheat on the CMP?'

'They told me to make sure that I was one of the last three on the CMP. If I did, I would help them with some of their medical experiments in space and my family would be looked after for life. It wasn't really that difficult. If someone makes you that sort of promise where I come from, you are happy to do whatever it takes to make it come true.'

'And when you got thrown out for cheating?'

Jia Li looked at the floor. 'The state kept me on the Shenzhou programme but took my name off the next mission list as punishment.'

'And your sponsors?'

'They offered the Chinese government the money they needed to build their segment of the ISS and helped put together a proposal to convince the US that they would be great ISS partners.'

'...As long as you were back on the ISS programme.'

'Exactly. But I didn't realise...'

'I think that is enough talking from you,' said Marat, pulling Jia Li backwards again.

'But how did you persuade Jia Li to get involved in your plan?' asked Michael, hoping that Marat wouldn't fly into a rage.

'She was easy to convince,' said Marat, with a thin, mean smile. 'China needs a cure for cancer and Jia Li needs her secrets to remain secret,' he said. 'She had no choice.'

'And if she didn't do what you wanted?'

'He would make public what happened on the CMP, expose my sponsors and shame my family,' said Jia Li, looking away. 'You have no idea what that would be like, Michael.'

Michael's brain couldn't process much more. He should be ecstatic that Jia Li was getting what she deserved, but he didn't feel like that. 'So, you blackmailed her?'

'You can use whichever words suit you,' said Marat. 'I did what I had to do. I found out about the experiment and made it possible for Jia Li to become an astronaut. Now you need to stop playing for time, Michael. Your crew members are not coming back, and Jia Li is now going to drink this.'

'Michael, help!' shouted Jia Li, forcing her left elbow down and into Marat's stomach.

'Arghh!' Marat doubled over, clutching his middle with one hand and keeping hold of the test tube in the other.

'He's not bothered about curing cancer. He's planning to *create* a cancer epidemic across the world with whatever's in the test tube and then Russia will release the antidote for sale. He's working with some political cell who want to make Russia powerful again,' rushed Jia Li as Marat pushed off the floor after her. 'I found the plans on his laptop.'

Something inside Michael snapped. He pushed his hand against the side of the module, sending him hurtling towards Marat.

'Get off me, you fool,' shouted Marat, stretching out his arms for the test tube that Michael had knocked out of his hand.

Michael grabbed a ledge on the ceiling and pulled. He had to get the test tube before Marat and before it smashed into the wall, releasing its menacing substance into the atmosphere.

'No!' shouted Marat, banging Michael into the wall as he forced past him.

Michael turned and stretched across the corridor, grabbing the test tube with the tips of his fingers and bringing it to his chest.

'Your time's up, Marat,' said Ralph, as the *Fortis* crew reappeared. 'We've talked to Mission Control and told them as much as they need to know for now. Michael and Jia Li can fill everyone in on the rest, but I don't think you'll be representing Russia in space again.'

Marat smiled. 'We will see, my friend. I think you may be underestimating the drive of our people to make Russia great again. I am only a small part of this. It will continue with or without me and if I cannot have the vaccine, neither will you.'

The attention now shifted to Jia Li. For the first time since Michael had known her, she looked like a fifteen-year-old girl who had just been grounded for life. Looking at the floor, she let her fringe cover as much of her creased face as possible.

'Yue...I mean...Jia Li. Without you, Marat wouldn't have been able to get this far and for that reason, you should go home too,' said Ralph.

Jia Li nodded and wiped her eyes. 'I understand.'

'But having talked to Jamie Matheson, it's clear we'd never have found out about Marat if you hadn't asked him to look at the full video footage. Whatever made you change your mind about going along with him, we are grateful and will talk more with Mission Control about what happens next.'

Michael had never seen a humble Jia Li before. She smiled and nodded to Ralph and each member of the *Fortis* crew. 'I thank you from the bottom of my heart,' she said, her voice wavering. 'As soon as I knew that my actions had caused Ralph's injury, I told Marat I wanted nothing more to do with his plans. I was horrified that he tampered with your suit, Buddy, and I made it my job to stop him. I had to pretend that I was going along with him until I could prove what he'd done. I realised that any shame on my family and me was nothing compared to that. I cannot seek your forgiveness, but your understanding.'

'But you took the test tube, stole Michael's ID and flicked the switch in *Harmony* node 2, didn't you?' said Buddy.

'Yes, I did.'

Steve laid his hand on Buddy's shoulder like a father would. 'Yes, Buddy. She did all of those things, but it was Jia Li who told Jamie to look at the video footage. She knew she'd incriminate herself, but she wanted to stop Marat.'

'What I don't get is how you knew when to flick the switch in *Harmony* node 2? I mean, any other timing and Ralph wouldn't have been touching it,' said Michael.

'We had a code word,' whispered Jia Li. 'I was just told to turn the power back on when he said the words "hard on your hands". Then I turned on the *Destiny* robotic workstation to slow you down whilst I returned to my sleep station.'

Ralph smiled. 'It's so simple, it's almost clever. You are really something, Marat. You're confined to your sleep station until further notice. Ru and Shen will make sure of it. Jia Li, you are to go and report back to them now. We'll talk more later.'

'That just leaves us then,' said Ralph, putting his arm around Steve, who did the same to Sarah, then Buddy and Michael.

In their astronaut circle, they looked at each other with a mixture of relief, disbelief and exhaustion.

'I've cleared it with Mission Control. I'm heading back tomorrow with Marat and Ru. Steve and Sarah are staying on to complete a further five months and...we wondered if you guys would want to extend your time and stay on with them?' said Ralph, looking straight at Michael and Buddy. 'You've both earned it.'

Michael had nowhere to look in this tight circle of people but the floor. No matter how good he became at being an astronaut, no matter how much older and more experienced he became, he'd always suck at this kind of thing.

'Er...thanks,' said Michael. 'That sounds amazing.'

'Yeah, it's a totally awesome offer,' added Buddy, pushing his fingers back through his hair. He looked at Michael with a shrug and half-smile.

'Er...could we have a few minutes to think about it, please?' said Michael, trying to work out if his head and his heart were together on this one.

'Sure,' said Ralph, breaking the circle. 'Take as long as you like, guys. This is a big deal. We'll go and wait in the *Destiny* lab. There's no way we're starting the experiment without you.'

Buddy and Michael were soon alone.

'What d'you think?' said Buddy, giving nothing away.

'Er...I dunno,' stuttered Michael. 'It's a bit hard to take it all in, isn't it? It's like we're in some sort of film or reality show where they keep throwing things at us to see how we react.'

'I suppose my mom would understand...and I guess I could wait a few more months to see my dad,' said Buddy, shrugging.

Michael paused before a smile trickled from the corners of his mouth. Could he stay up here? Could he be an astronaut for another five months? He looked at the organised jumble around him and then at Buddy. 'I guess we'd better ask Mission Control to send up some more caramel cookies and salt and vinegar crisps on the next supply craft then.'

As Sarah put the final sample of XO3 in the last test tube, the *Destiny* lab fell silent.

Michael ran through the whirlwind events of the past week. He'd been the first child in space, the first on the ISS, visited the moon and stopped an international sabotage attempt. And, if that wasn't enough, in just a few hours he'd find out if he was part of the most important medical breakthrough in decades. He nodded. 'If you don't need me anymore, I've got an important call home to make. Goodnight, guys,' he said, pushing off the wall and gliding silently away.

Magnificent Me, Magnificent You The Grand Canyon
Dawattie Basdeo, Angela Cutler
A treasure filled story of discovery with a range of inspiring fun exercises, activities, songs and games for children aged 6 to 11.
Paperback: 978-1-78279-819-4

Q is for Question
An ABC of Philosophy
Tiffany Poirier
An illustrated non-fiction philosophy book to help children aged 8 to 11 discover, debate and articulate thought-provoking, open-ended questions about existence, free will and happiness.
Hardcover: 978-1-84694-183-2

Relax Kids: How to be Happy
52 positive activities for children
Marneta Viegas
Fun activities to bring the family together.
Paperback: 978-1-78279-162-1

Rise of the Shadow Stealers
The Firebird Chronicles
Daniel Ingram-Brown
Memories are going missing. Can Fletcher and Scoop unearth their own lost history and save the Storyteller's treasure from the shadows?
Paperback: 978-1-78099-694-3 ebook: 978-1-78099-693-6

Readers of ebooks can buy or view any of these bestsellers by clicking on the live link in the title. Most titles are published in paperback and as an ebook. Paperbacks are available in traditional bookshops. Both print and ebook formats are available online.

Find more titles and sign up to our readers' newsletter at http://www.johnhuntpublishing.com/children-and-young-adult Follow us on Facebook at https://www.facebook.com/JHPChildren and Twitter at https://twitter.com/JHPChildren